"I...I'll miss you,"
she whispered softly

It wasn't what Daphne had intended to say, but she could find no other way to show Carlos that she had valued his strength and protection during the past few days.

Carlos flicked an eyebrow satirically. "I thought you'd be glad to have a bed to yourself for a night," he drawled.

"Please don't make fun. I...I mean it. I'll miss you." Daphne felt herself move toward him, her lips parting. Suddenly, on a heavy sigh, he moved, too, possessing her lips hungrily. Then, just as suddenly, Carlos pushed her away.

"Was that what you wanted?" he asked harshly.

"I...I don't know," Daphne gasp

"So if you don't know what you don't try a trick like that again rebuked her coldly.

FLORA KIDD
is also the author of these

Harlequin Presents

and these
Harlequin Romances

Many of these titles are available at your local bookseller.

For a free catalogue listing all available Harlequin Romances
and Harlequin Presents, send your name and address to:

HARLEQUIN READER SERVICE
1440 South Priest Drive, Tempe, AZ 85281
Canadian address: Stratford, Ontario N5A 6W2

FLORA KIDD

makebelieve marriage

Harlequin Books

TORONTO • LONDON • LOS ANGELES • AMSTERDAM
SYDNEY • HAMBURG • PARIS • STOCKHOLM • ATHENS • TOKYO

Harlequin Presents first edition August 1982
ISBN 0-373-10520-7

Original hardcover edition published in 1982
by Mills & Boon Limited

CHAPTER ONE

AGAINST the blue-black night sky the lights of Acapulco glittered, competing with the diamond sparkle of a myriad stars. The air was warm and calm and in the bushes, which crowded about a handsome house built in the Spanish style on a hill overlooking the beautiful light-reflecting bay, cicadas chanted their night-song to the accompaniment of the music which throbbed out through long open windows.

Elsa Thomas, the actress whose dramatic films, torrid love affairs and four stormy marriages had entertained the public for more than twenty years, was giving a party, and the spacious *salón* of the house was crowded with many well-known film actors and actresses, film directors and producers, young and hopeful starlets, hangers-on and even a few gatecrashers.

Clothes were informal and varied. Women were wearing everything from brightly coloured caftans to low-cut slinky evening gowns. Some were wearing shorts and halter tops. Others were wearing see-through chiffon pantaloons with bra tops. There was a great deal of smooth, suntanned skin on show.

Most of the men were wearing lightweight casual slacks and dressy long-sleeved shirts. Some shirts were typically Mexican, loose and collarless with deep slits for openings, and were worn with tasselled sashes. Other shirts were tucked, pleated or embroidered, high-necked in the Chinese fashion or open to the waist to display chains and pendants.

Only one man was wearing a conventional shirt and tie with a suit. Of medium height with very broad shoulders, he leaned against a wall just inside one of the long arched windows which opened on to a patio. His hands were thrust casually into the trouser pockets of his light grey alpaca suit and he was watching all that was going on in the room with hard black eyes, a slightly cynical twist at one corner of his mouth.

While two young women dressed in formal black and white maid's uniforms moved about with trays full of cocktails and tasty titbits of sea-food, Elsa Thomas was holding court in the middle of the room. She talked vivaciously to everyone who approached her, her white hands gesturing all the time so that her rings caught the light and flashed ostentatiously. Her blonde hair was dressed with casual elegance, her blue eyes sparkled between their thick mascaraed lashes and she laughed a lot, her painted lips parting over tiny cat-like teeth. The laugh itself was coarse and loud, thought the man who was leaning against the wall, and he wondered vaguely why no one had ever told her not to laugh in public, because when she did she destroyed immediately the image she had been at such pains to create over the years, the image of serene yet mysterious female beauty.

Feeling suddenly suffocated by the theatrical atmosphere of the room, sickened by the false gaiety of the people in it, he lunged away from the wall and turned sharply to go out on to the patio. He collided immediately with one of the maids who was entering the room with a tray laden with full glasses, and the tray spun from her hands. Glasses crashed to the floor, spilling their contents over the thick carpet. People stopped talking and turned to stare.

The maid, a tall slim young woman with golden hair cut short and falling in a thick curving wave across her forehead, stared in consternation at the mess on the floor, then raised her head to glare accusingly at the man who had walked into her.

'*Lo siento, señorita,*' he said in a soft gruff voice, but she did not understand what he had said and continued to stare at him, not so much annoyed with him now as fascinated by his unusual colouring and handsome profile.

'You little fool!' Elsa's voice shrilled spitefully as she advanced towards the maid. 'Why don't you look where you're going?'

'I did look where I was going,' retorted the maid, her eyes, which were the same colour as Elsa's but more widely spaced, flashing angrily. 'It was his fault.' She pointed at the man in the suit.

'She's right,' the man said in English, his voice drawling slightly, a faint self-mocking smile curving his wide thin-lipped mouth. 'I wasn't looking where I was going. You'll let me pay for the damage, of course.'

'It's kind of you to offer, darling,' Elsa's face changed miraculously and she smiled up at him as she slid a bare lightly-tanned arm through his, 'but I can't let you take the blame for what this silly little bitch has done.' She turned on the maid, her face hardening, and snapped viciously, 'Well, don't just stand there—do something about the mess you've made. Clear it up!'

'No!' The word rang out defiantly as the maid faced up to the actress, and the people who were nearest and who had lost interest in the scene stopped talking again to turn and stare.

'Then get out!' Elsa spat the words out dramatically and raised a long graceful arm to point to the open window. 'Do you hear me?' she asked, unnecessarily, because her voice was loud and clear and could no doubt be heard by anyone who was in the garden. 'Get out! Go on, leave now. I've had enough of you and your insolence!' She turned towards the group of people who were watching and admiring the performance by their favourite film star. 'After all I've done to help her,' she complained, her voice breaking slightly, tears welling in her beautiful eyes, 'taking her in and giving her a job when I found her, my brother's only child. She was poor and out of work, so I offered her a home with me, and in return she's tried to come between Mitch and me, to destroy our marriage. You see what happens when you're charitable to a poor relation. . . .'

'Liar! Hypocrite!' Daphne Thomas's voice shook with anger as she cried out the words and everyone gasped, enjoying to the full the drama of the scene between aunt and niece. But Daphne wasn't acting. She meant everything she said, felt it from the heart. 'I've had enough, too, of you and your ... your so-called charity and your sleazy hypocritical friends!' Her eyes flashed contemptuously as they flicked over the fascinated audience. With another accusing glare at the man who had caused the accident she spun round and left the room by the window through which she had entered it.

Into the soft melting darkness of the night Daphne ran, across the patio and into another part of the house. She ran up a narrow stairway to the servants' quarters and entered her room. Switching on the light, she went over to a closet and taking out a battered suitcase heaved it on to the bed, opened it and began to pack her clothes into it.

She packed quickly and methodically, not allowing her thoughts to wander from the course on which they were set. This time she was really going to leave. She didn't know where she was going, but she was leaving Elsa's employment for good. She couldn't stand living with and working for her aunt any longer. She couldn't stand Mitchell Gardner, Elsa's fourth husband, any longer either, with his wandering hands and eyes and his suggestion that she should become his mistress here in this house, under Elsa's nose.

When the suitcase was packed she took off the maid's uniform and dressed in white slacks, sleeveless green shirt and a white blazer jacket. Picking up her suitcase and handbag, she left the

room, leaving the house by the door she had
entered and walking along the driveway which
wound down to the road. Behind her music and
voices wafted out into the still dark night as the
party continued.

Daphne suspected that Elsa would have liked
her to have played the scene in the *salón* a little
differently. No doubt Elsa would have liked her
only niece, to whom she had apparently been so
generous, to have pleaded with her, asking to be
allowed to stay and work for her. And then Elsa
would have shown her admirers how loving and
forgiving she could be. She would have put on
another act, pretending to forgive the young
woman whom she had accused of attempting to
steal her husband away from her. Daphne's lips
curved in a wry grimace. Whoever would want
Mitchell Gardner after Elsa had finished with
him?

She was half way down the driveway when a
figure stepped out of the oleander bushes and
walked towards her.

'Daphne, you're not really leaving?' Mitchell
Gardner's voice was slurred by the liquor he had
drunk and he swayed slightly on his feet as he
stood over her, blocking the way, the white silk of
his shirt glimmering faintly in the darkness.

'Yes, I am.' She waited warily, wondering
which way to step round him.

'But I can't let you go,' he muttered, reaching
out and grasping her shoulders. 'You've got to
stay—I need you. Elsa didn't mean what she said
back there. You know what her temper is like.

She'll have got over it by morning and she'll expect you to be there to dress her hair and wait on her.' His hands tightened on her shoulders and he drew her towards him. 'Daphne, honey, don't go. Stay with me. I want you.'

'No, no!' She dropped her suitcase so that her two hands were free to push him away. 'I don't want to stay. Oh, let me go, let me go!' she cried, kicking at his shins, hating the touch of his hands as they slid over her body and the smell of his liquor-laden breath as his mouth came down on hers. The feel of his slack wet lips on hers turned her into a fury and she struggled, twisting and turning, hitting at him with both hands, scratching at his face, guessing that if she couldn't get away from him he would force himself upon her there in the bushes beside the driveway.

Suddenly there was light and noise. Tyres squealed on tarmac as a car came to an abrupt stop, but Mitchell didn't seem to notice it and continued to hold her tightly. Still struggling to free herself from his hateful embrace, Daphne heard a car door slam. Then it seemed that Mitchell was lifted away from her and she saw him go staggering backwards to fall down at the side of the driveway. By the light of the headlamps she recognised the driver of the car. He was the man in the suit who had collided with her in the *salón*.

'Are you all right?' he asked.

'Yes, I am now,' she whispered, wiping her hand across her lips in an attempt to wipe away the feel of Mitchell's lips. 'Thank you,' she added.

'You're welcome.' He paused, looking down at her with eyes as black as coal in his shadowy face. 'I guess I owed you something for causing trouble for you at the house just now. Can I drive you somewhere?'

Groans from Mitchell drew her glance towards the side of the driveway, where he was lying on the ground.

'What did you do to Mitchell?' she asked the other man.

'Sobered him up a little, that's all.'

'I hope you haven't hurt him.'

'Listen, lady,' he drawled with a touch of impatience, 'I got the impression that you weren't too happy with his attentions when I came along or I wouldn't have interfered. But if you want to stay around and comfort him, that's okay. I'll be on my way.' He stepped towards the car.

Out of the corners of her eyes Daphne saw that Mitchell was trying to stand up, and she panicked.

'No, I don't want to comfort him,' she said hastily, picking up her case and going over to the car. 'And I would like a lift into the town, please.'

'Then get in,' ordered the man in the suit crisply, opening one of the car doors. 'Give me your case and I'll put it in the back seat.'

'Hey, Daphne, where the hell do you think you're going?' demanded Mitchell as she slid into the passenger seat.

Doors were slammed. The man in the suit slid

behind the steering wheel and slammed the door beside him. The engine started. Tyres squealing again, the vehicle leapt forward along the drive, past the swaying, shouting Mitchell.

'I'm Carlos Reynolds,' said the man who was driving. 'Your name is?'

'Daphne Thomas.'

'So you're really related to Elsa.'

'Yes, although recently I've been wishing that I wasn't.' She paused, took a deep shaking breath and added fiercely, 'I wish she hadn't gone to Wales last year and found me, and I wish I'd never accepted her invitation to live with her and be her personal maid!'

'Was it true, what she said? Were you out of work when she found you?' he asked.

'No, it wasn't. I'm a hairdresser and I was working in a beauty salon in Swansea. She came back to the town where she was born for a publicity stunt—celebrity returns to her roots to show she remembers her family and her poor beginnings. I'm the only surviving member of the family. My father, who was much older than Elsa, was killed in a coalmining accident years ago,' she explained.

'And the rest of it, the bit about coming between her and her husband. Is that true?' he asked.

'No, it isn't,' she replied in fierce denial. They were on the road now and she could see the city's light twinkling ahead of them. 'I'd be glad if you would drop me off in the *zócalo*,' she added politely.

'What will you do there?'

'Find somewhere to stay the night.'

'And tomorrow? What then?'

'I'll look for a job.'

'Do you speak Spanish?' he asked.

'Not much. Nor do I understand it. I haven't been in the country very long.'

'But you think you'll get a job knowing only English.'

'Well, it shouldn't be too hard to find work in a hotel beauty salon where most of the guests are English-speaking,' she argued.

'Don't you plan to return to your own country?'

'I can't afford to yet. I don't have enough money for the air fare.'

He made no further comment and the car surged along the Costera Miguel Alémán, following the curve of the extensive bay. A row of glittering high-rise buildings came into view, the luxury beach hotels where swarms of holiday-makers from other parts of Mexico and from the United States stayed every year. Soon they turned into the *zócalo*, the plaza in the centre of the town, and Daphne asked Carlos Reynolds to stop again so that she could get out. But he didn't seem to hear her and the car nosed its way through the night-time traffic, past the extraordinary Cathedral, gold, white and blue, with its twin Byzantine towers and mosque-like dome, and along a street which led to the fast super-highway, the most direct route to Mexico City.

'I asked you to stop by the Cathedral,' she said,

turning urgently towards him, 'but I don't think you heard me.'

'I heard you,' he replied coolly, and turning the car on to the highway he put his foot down on the accelerator. The engine responded at once and the vehicle seemed to fly along.

'Where are you going? Where are you taking me?' she exclaimed, really worried now.

'This road goes, as I'm sure you know, to the capital,' he said smoothly.

'But I don't want to go there. Please take me back to Acapulco.'

Again he didn't reply and Daphne felt panic prick her.

'Oh, I should have guessed,' she complained bitterly. 'You're no better than the other men who go to Elsa's parties. You're no better than Mitchell, after all. Please stop and let me out. I don't want to go any further with you. I refuse to be kidnapped by you!'

'I'm not kidnapping you,' he retorted. 'I'm trying to help you. It's my fault you had to leave Elsa's house tonight, my fault you don't have a job any more, so I feel responsible for what happens to you, and I can't let you stay alone in some cheap hotel or walk the streets looking for a job. Someone might take advantage of you. You're safe with me.'

'But you shouldn't feel responsible for me,' she argued. 'I've been thinking of leaving Elsa for some time. I don't want your help. I can take care of myself.'

He didn't reply and the car roared on the road which was climbing steadily towards the Sierra

Madre del Sur. Flying insects attracted by the light of the headlamps zoomed towards the windscreen and collided with the hard glass in the way she had collided with the man at her side, thought Daphne fancifully. Watching their wings flattened against the glass, seeing their slender bodies splatter against it, she bit her lip. Was that how she would end her life, broken and squashed by the hard, merciless treatment of other people? She glanced sideways uneasily at the dark bulk of her companion.

'How long does it take to get to Mexico City?' she asked.

'On this road between five and six hours. But we won't go all the way tonight. In a while we'll reach Iguala. I know an inn near there where we can stay for the night.'

'But I don't want to stay the night with you in Iguala or any other place,' she said desperately. 'Oh, please won't you listen to me? I want to go back to Acapulco. I don't want to go with you.'

'You have no choice,' he replied coldly. 'I'm not stopping to let you out. Where would you go if I did? We're well beyond the town now. And I'm not returning to Acapulco—I've had enough of it. So sit back and relax. I've taken over the responsibility of finding somewhere for you to stay for the night and tomorrow I'll help you find a job. It's the least I can do for you.'

'You're really expecting a lot from me,' she grumbled, although she was doing as he had suggested, she was sitting back in the comfortable bucket seat and was relaxing because she had found quite suddenly that she was exhausted. The strain of the past few weeks living with Elsa and Mitchell, the drama of the scene in the *salón*, the struggle with Mitchell on the driveway, seemed to have sapped all her strength so that she had none left to fight this man who said he had taken over responsibility of finding her somewhere to stay for the night.

'Am I? In what way am I expecting a lot from you?' He sounded surprised.

'You're expecting me to trust you, yet we met less than an hour ago. Why should I trust you more than Mitchell Gardner?'

'Mmm, I catch your drift,' he drawled. 'But you're a little late thinking of that, aren't you? All I can say to put your mind at rest and in recommendation of myself is that I'm not one of Elsa Thomas's pet men. Nor am I hoping to be her next husband. Nor am I an actor or in any way connected with the film business.'

'Then what were you doing at Elsa's party? Did you gatecrash it?'

'No. I was invited, by Elsa herself. I met her yesterday, and she asked me to call in at her house this evening.' He paused, then added, 'If I hadn't delayed my departure to go to her party I'd have been well on my way by now.'

Daphne glanced at him again, wishing she could see him properly, trying to remember what he looked like and recalling a tough square-chinned face weathered to the colour of golden-brown leather, fathomless black eyes and surprisingly, with those Mexican dark eyes, a lot of casually cut tawny-brown hair, only a few shades darker than her own.

'Where is home?' she asked curiously.

'Right now it's on the Fontaine Ranch, near Micatepec,' he replied.

'I've only been in Mexico for a month, so you must excuse me if I seem ignorant,' she said lightly, 'but I've no idea where Mica ... Mica ... you see, I can't even say it,' she complained, with a little laugh. 'Is it in Mexico?'

'It is, in the state of Veracruz, on the eastern side of the country.'

'I know Carlos is Spanish for Charles, but Reynolds doesn't sound like a Mexican name. It's English or even Welsh in origin. I mean, most Mexicans have Spanish last names, don't they?' she said.

'Many do,' he agreed. 'But some have Italian, German, Japanese, Chinese, Indian, Scottish, Irish, English and Welsh names. French too. Like most nations, Mexicans are a mixed-up lot. For example, the area around Micatepec was settled by some French immigrants in the last century and the ranch where I live and work has been owned by the Fontaine family ever since then. Some years ago the owner of the ranch offered the job of manager to my father, John Reynolds, a cowboy from Texas. When he took the job my father met my Mexican mother and married her.' He paused, then added with a touch of mockery, 'I hope that satisfies you as to the origin of my hybrid name.'

'Yes, it does,' Daphne replied seriously. 'Thank

you for telling me. I've never met anyone who worked on a ranch before.'

There was a short silence, then she asked,

'How old are you?'

'Thirty-four. Why do you want to know?'

'Oh, I'm just naturally curious about people.'

'How old are you?' he asked, and there was a suggestion of laughter in his voice.

'Almost twenty-three.'

There was another silence. They were nearer to the mountains and she could see sharp dark peaks outlined against the star-bright sky. Nearer at hand the lights of a town twinkled. Iguala? The muscles in her stomach tensed nervously. What was she doing trapped in this car and at the mercy of its driver, a man she didn't know? Had she jumped out of the frying pan into the fire when she had jumped so quickly into the car to escape from Mitchell?

But what would have happened if she hadn't got into the car? A shudder went through her as she imagined how Mitchell might have behaved. His pride hurt because she had rejected him and he had then been hit by another man, he would have made her suffer in some way, she could be sure of that. No, she was better off sitting here beside the unknown quantity who was Carlos Reynolds than she would have been if she had stayed with Mitchell, the devil she knew and had managed to avoid for the past month.

She sighed wearily and closed her eyes, her thoughts drifting back to the day when Elsa had turned up at the beauty salon in Swansea and had asked if a Daphne Thomas worked there. She had been thrilled because her father's famous, fabulous younger sister had sought her out. It had been wonderful to be wanted suddenly by a beautiful, wealthy relative who had seemed to care about what happened to her. Elsa had dazzled her, Daphne could see that now. Appearing like a fairy godmother in the story of Cinderella, the actress had waved her magic wand and had whisked her niece away from the Welsh seaport and across the Atlantic to Hollywood, to live there in luxurious surroundings. In return Daphne had only to be Elsa's personal maid.

For the first few months everything had been fine while Elsa had been busy shooting a new film at the studios in Hollywood. It was when the film-making had ended and they had moved to the house Elsa owned in Acapulco, where Mitchell Gardner had joined them, that life had become complicated for Daphne. Slightly younger than Elsa, handsome in a rakish way, Mitchell had once been a good actor with a great future in films. Then he had been cast in a role opposite Elsa and had fallen in love with her. Bewitched by her beauty, he had divorced his wife and had left his two young children so that he could marry the film star.

That had happened three years ago, and exactly when the relationship had begun to go sour Daphne didn't know, but she hadn't been in Acapulco long before she had discovered that Elsa and Mitchell shouted at each other most of the day, creating an atmosphere of tension in the house which no servant could put up with for long. She had also discovered that Mitchell drank too much and when he was drunk he became maudlin, seeking her out to tell her his troubles and later boasting to Elsa that her niece was much more co-operative and sympathetic than she was, implying all the time that his relationship with Daphne was much closer than it had been, hoping possibly to rouse Elsa's jealousy because he knew she had become bored with him.

Oh, she was glad she had escaped, thought Daphne. No matter what came of this new adventure she was glad that in the morning she wouldn't wake up with a feeling of dread wondering how she was going to avoid Mitchell's suggestive caresses. Her head slid sideways, her slim young body went slack and she dozed, soothed by the undemanding silence of the man who was driving, cradled by the comfort of the seat.

The slowing down of the car's engine wakened her and she opened her eyes to the soft glow of lamplight casting the shadows of leaves on thick white walls. Then the engine stopped, and rubbing a crick which had developed in the side of her neck, Daphne turned towards Carlos.

'Where are we?' she asked.

'In the courtyard of the inn near Iguala I was telling you about.'

He opened his door, got out of the car and slammed the door shut. In a few moments he appeared at the door beside her to open it. As the door swung back and the interior light came on again she hesitated about getting out, still distrusting him.

'*Que pasa?* What's wrong?' he demanded coldly.

'I . . . I'm not sure,' she muttered.

'Look, it's late, past midnight, and I'm ready for bed,' he replied curtly. 'Come on, get out and we'll go and find what accommodation the inn has to offer.' She didn't move, so he bent again to look in at her. 'Or perhaps you would prefer to sleep in the car,' he drawled acidly.

Still she didn't move, so muttering something in Spanish, he withdrew and swung the door shut. He walked away, and Daphne stared at the shadow leaves fluttering on the white wall in front of the car. He had gone away and had left her to her own devices, free to sleep in the car if she wished; free to walk out to the highway to hitch a lift back to Acapulco.

But hitch-hiking was something Daphne knew it wasn't wise to do in this country, so she wasn't going to make any move in that direction. And it was hot in the car now that the air-conditioning had been turned off, so hot she could feel the sweat breaking out on her skin. Oh, what a mess she was in! She didn't even have a handkerchief to wipe the sweat from her brow and she was longing for a drink, a long thirst-quenching drink, and a bath or a shower. If she went into the inn she might be able to get both a drink and a wash.

Slowly she opened the door of the car and stepped out. She opened the rear door and took out her suitcase, then looked around the court-yard. Light glowed beyond a curved archway, so she went towards it and saw the entrance to the inn. Cautiously she pushed a thick wooden door open and stepped into a high square hallway, dimly lit and cool. In spite of the lateness of the hour the clerk behind the reception desk was smiling and deferential, nodding his head at whatever Carlos Reynolds was saying to him. Both of them looked round when they heard Daphne enter.

'So it is done,' said Carlos easily, coming towards her. He carried a zipped overnight bag in one hand and in the other a room key with a tab on it. 'We have a room for the night,' he added.

'One room?' she queried uncertainly.

'*Si*, one room. A double, the only one left. This way.'

Slinging the overnight bag to the hand which held the key, he took her suitcase from her and began to walk towards an elegant wrought-iron staircase that led up to a gallery which ran round the four walls of the hallway. Daphne followed him.

'But we need two rooms,' she whispered, glancing back at the clerk. He was watching them, but when he saw she was looking at him he bowed and smiled.

'*Buenas noches, señora,*' he said.

'There is only one,' said Carlos imperturbably as he went up the stairs. 'And it's usual for husband and wife to share a room.'

'*Wife?* You told him I'm your wife?' Daphne exclaimed loudly as they reached the top of the stairs and he turned to face her.

'Don't shout!' he rebuked her sharply, frowning

at her. 'Keep your voice down—people are sleeping behind those doors. I had to make up some story about you so that you could share the room with me, and it prevented any trouble about your identity.'

'But I don't want to share a room with you!' she hissed.

'Go back to the car, then,' he retorted, and still carrying her suitcase he strode along the gallery to a door at the far end and inserted the key in its lock. The door opened and he disappeared into the room.

Daphne glanced down the stairs. The clerk was at the bottom of them peering up at her. He began to walk up the stairs. He said something to her in Spanish, and she replied with one of the few phrases she knew in Spanish, shaking her head.

'*No entiendo, señor.*'

His dark eyes narrowed suspiciously and he came on up the stairs. She didn't like the way he was looking at her, so she turned on her heel and hurried along the gallery to the door through which Carlos had disappeared. It was closed. Glancing back, Daphne saw the clerk standing at the top of the stairs watching her. She knocked on the door, and to her relief it opened at once. The expression on Carlo's tough, square-jawed face was cynical.

'I guessed you'd come sooner or later,' he drawled dryly, and stood back to let her in, closing the door after her.

The room was furnished with a big double bed covered in white. On the floor was a thick carpet patterned in a mosaic of black and white. Chests of golden wood glowed in the soft light of two bedside lamps. In one of the thick walls a mirrored door stood partially open, and beyond it the tiles of a bathroom wall gleamed.

Daphne glanced at Carlos. He had already taken off his suit jacket and was in the process of taking off his shirt. Muscles rippled beneath the silk smoothness of the tanned skin of his back as he tossed the shirt casually on to a blanket chest beneath the window. Stepping over to his overnight bag, he took out a toilet bag and some cotton shorts. He turned and paused when he noticed her.

'Take your jacket off, make yourself at home,' he said. 'I won't be long in the bathroom, then you can have it.'

'This room is very luxurious,' she commented. 'And I can't afford to stay here.'

'But I can,' he replied coolly, and began to walk towards the bathroom door.

'I've never shared a room with a man before,' she went on hurriedly. 'Perhaps ... perhaps I could sleep on the floor.'

From the doorway of the bathroom he gave her a glinting sardonic glance.

'You can do whatever you wish,' he drawled, and going into the bathroom closed the door firmly.

In a way his cool indifference towards her was reassuring, Daphne thought as she slid her jacket off and hung it in the closet. It meant, surely, that he wasn't interested in her as a woman but merely as someone he had decided to help. Sitting down in a small cushioned armchair, she took off her sandals and leaning back stared at the bed. King-sized, big enough to sleep four people quite comfortably, she thought. Big enough for her and Carlos Reynolds to sleep in without ever being near each other. But perhaps, now that she had suggested it, he might sleep on the floor. She yawned suddenly and uncontrollably. Oh, it would be good to stretch out between cool sheets and to sink down into the oblivion of sleep for a few hours.

The bathroom door opened and he came into the room wearing only the sleeping shorts. Going over to the closet, he hung his trousers on a hanger, then went to the bed and pulled back the top cover, rolling it down to the foot of the bed. Lifting the top sheet, he lay down on the bed and settled his head on a pillow.

'*Buenas noches,*' he murmured, and stretching out a hand switched off the bedside lamp nearest to him.

In the bathroom Daphne showered quickly and rubbed her hair as dry as she could. She dressed in her nightgown and returned to the bedroom. Carlos Reynolds was hidden in shadow and after hanging up her slacks Daphne walked over to the other side of the bed. She lay down quietly under the sheet, folding it down to her waist, then switched off the other lamp. Sleep swooped over her almost as swiftly as darkness swooped across the room, blotting out all her anxieties.

CHAPTER TWO

DAPHNE woke up suddenly and sensed immediately that she was in a strange bed. Opening her eyes, she stared wonderingly for a few moments at a narrow window set in a thick white wall. Through the window she could see the bright hot blue of the Mexican sky. Sunlight slanted into the room, glinting on mirrors and gilding the golden wood of the furniture. On a heavy oak blanket chest beneath the window was an open zipped overnight bag. Beside it was a man's grey shirt and a dark red tie. Both of them had been tossed there last night by the man who had brought her to this inn, and the fact that they were still there meant he was still about somewhere.

Cautiously she turned her head and glanced across the bed, feeling relief rush through her when she saw that no one was there. The only signs that she had had company in the bed was the rumpled sheet and pillow. Sitting up, she leaned back against the padded headboard. She felt wonderfully rested. Strangely, she felt secure too. Why? Was it because Carlos Reynolds had done what he had promised he would do? He had found her a place to stay for the night without demanding anything in return. Dared she hope he would carry out the rest of his promise and help her to find a job?

Pushing aside the sheet, she slipped from the bed, visited the bathroom and then dressed in a simple sleeveless cotton dress patterned in blue and white. She packed the white pant suit and blouse she had worn the previous night in her suitcase and locked it. Taking her wallet out of her handbag, she counted how much money she possessed.

About a thousand *pesos* in cash. Not much, and it wouldn't last very long. Maybe she had left Elsa's house too hastily. Maybe she should go back and apologise for having been rude. *No*. A shudder went through her. She couldn't ever go back to live in that unpleasant environment. She would rather be free and live precariously from day to day than be beholden to Elsa any longer.

The door of the room opened and she turned quickly. Carlos Reynolds, dressed in the same grey suit but with a different dark blue shirt which was open at the neck, stepped inside and closed the door.

'*Buenos dias*,' he said politely.' I hope you slept well. Would you like some breakfast? It's almost eight-fifteen and I would like to be on the road by nine.'

In a pleasant sunlit dining room she sat opposite to him at a table set with a red and white checked tablecloth and studied him over the top edge of her menu card, her glance dropping quickly to the printed words on the card when he looked up from his menu and straight at her.

There was something calculating in the expression of those opaque eyes which stiffened her backbone. She felt she was being looked over and studied for imperfections as if she were a prize bull . . . no, a prize cow, she corrected herself with a little grin.

'*Buenos dias, señora y señor.*' The waiter was young and handsome with flashing brown eyes and a tawny skin and was wearing a red sash around the waist of his loose white cotton shirt. '*Que desean ustedes?*'

Daphne glanced at Carlos. She was a little disconcerted at being addressed as *señora* again, and she hadn't understood the rest of the waiter's remarks.

'What would you like to eat?' Carlos asked.

'I would like an omelette, some orange juice and coffee, please,' she said. He spoke to the waiter in rapid Spanish and the young man went away.

'You should try to learn some Spanish while you're in this country,' said Carlos, and she looked across at him again. He was studying her again, his eyes narrowed, and she had the feeling he didn't altogether approve of her. 'Didn't you pick up any phrases when you were living in Acapulco? I noticed that Elsa employed some Mexicans to work for her.'

'None of them stayed long enough for me to get to know any of them,' she replied.

'Why was that? Didn't she pay them enough?'

'It wasn't a question of pay. She and Mitchell were always fighting.' She noticed the surprised lift of his eyebrows and added quickly, 'Oh, I don't mean physically. They didn't hit one another . . . although sometimes Elsa threw things at Mitchell . . . I mean they shouted at each other, all the time, called each other names and accused each other of all sorts of lies and infidelities.' She made a grimace of distaste. 'It was most unpleasant, and the servants Elsa hired didn't like it, so they left. One week there was no help at all and I did everything—the cooking, the cleaning as well as waiting on Elsa personally.'

The waiter came with glasses of orange juice and a pot of coffee. As he set her juice in front of her Daphne said rather selfconsciously,

'*Muchas gracias.*'

'*De nada, señora.* You are welcome, *señora*,' he replied with an appreciative smile, and departed.

'It's very disconcerting being called *señora* when I'm not married,' Daphne complained as she picked up her glass of juice.

'Wouldn't you like to be married?' Carlos asked casually.

'Yes, I would. Most normal women hope to marry some day. I'm just waiting for the right man to come along and ask me,' she said lightly. She sipped some juice and looked at him again, studying him stealthily from beneath her lashes while he looked away across the room at something she couldn't see. Tough, tough as leather with his sun-weathered skin, hard black eyes, beaky nose and straight controlled lips, he looked as if he had never had a tender feeling or sentimental thought in his life, and she was curious suddenly about his personal life. 'Are you married?' she ventured.

The glance of the dark eyes swerved to her face. There was a glint in their depths.

'*Si*, I'm married. To you,' he drawled mockingly. 'Have you forgotten we stayed the night here as husband and wife?'

'But that was just pretence, a masquerade marriage,' she argued. 'And you could be married, legally married, for all I know.'

The glint in his eyes seemed to grow more menacing as he stared at her, the long line of his lips taking on a downward curve.

'You believe that I would sign you into a hotel register as my wife if I were already married to another woman?' he queried, his voice soft and silky.

'Some men do it all the time,' she retorted, refusing to be intimidated.

'But I'm not one of them,' he replied coldly.

'So how was I to know that?' Daphne challenged.

'Did I attempt to rape you last night when we slept in the same bed?' he retaliated.

'No.' To her annoyance she felt colour rise in her cheeks.

'So, there is your answer.' He picked up the coffee pot and poured hot dark liquid into the thick pottery mugs the waiter had brought. 'I have no legal wife at the present time,' he said slowly. He set the coffee pot down and looked across at her. Now his eyes were opaque, completely without light, mysterious. 'What would you say if I asked you to marry me and make the masquerade a reality?' he drawled.

Shocked into temporary silence by the question, Daphne stared across the table at the rock-jawed, hardbitten face. Black eyes stared back at her steadily. The waiter came with the omelettes, a basket of fresh rolls and a dish of butter, set them down and departed.

'This wouldn't be the job you were going to help me to find today, would it?' Daphne asked at last. Although her voice was a little croaky she thought she managed to seem cool and collected, as if proposals of marriage from strange men happened to her every day of her life.

'You can think of it that way, if you wish,' he replied calmly, picking up his fork and beginning to eat as if he hadn't said anything unusual.

'But why ask a woman you've only just met to marry you?' she asked. 'Surely there are women in this country you know much better than you know me who would be only too glad to marry you? You seem to be financially secure and you're . . . well, you're not bad looking.'

'*Muchas gracias*,' he drawled, giving her a mocking glance as he bowed slightly. 'It's true there are women I know better than I know you, but none of them is suitable to be my wife.'

'And what makes you think I'm suitable after such a short acquaintance?' she challenged him.

He scooped up the last of his omelette, ate it, set his fork down and drank some coffee before he replied. Then he put his folded arms on the table and leaned towards her.

'You don't have much money, not enough to
pay your air fare back to England,' he said quietly.
'Not enough to support you for much more than
two days if you have to pay for somewhere to stay
the night and eat decent meals as well. Right?'

'Yes, that's true, but. . . .' She broke off and
gave him an intent stare. 'How do you know how
much money I have?' she demanded suspiciously.

'You told me yourself you don't have the air
fare,' he replied smoothly. 'And this morning
while you still slept I examined the contents of
your wallet.'

'Oh, of all the nerve!' she exclaimed angrily,
glaring at him.

'Shush! Be quiet!' he ordered. 'Everyone is
looking at you.'

Daphne glanced round the room. Heads were
turned her way. She looked back at Carlos. He
was watching her, his face impassive.

'You had no right to open my handbag,' she
said in a loud whisper.

'As I was saying,' he went on, completely
ignoring her remarks, 'you don't have much
money. You are an alien in this country and
cannot speak or understand the official language,
yet you think you can get a job. You have no
friends or relatives to turn to for help, unless you
go back to Elsa.' He paused and gave her a sharp
questioning glance. 'Do you want to go back to
her?'

'No. Never!' She said vehemently. 'But if I do
need help I can always go to the British Embassy
in Mexico City or. . . .'

'I am trying to tell you why I think you are suitable to be my wife,' he interrupted her sharply. 'You could be polite and listen to what I have to say before making a remark. To continue. It appears that you are single and as far as I can tell you are not promised to marry anyone, yet you would like to be married and are only waiting for Mr Right to come along.'

'May I say something now?' asked Daphne, glowering at him from beneath her eyebrows.

'*Si*, you may.'

'I know I said I would like to be married and that I was waiting for the right man to come along, but I didn't mean I would accept the first proposal I received. I was ... well, I was making a sort of joke when I said that. There would have to be a good reason for me to marry.'

'What reason?'

'I'd have to know the man and like him before I even began to consider his proposal and. . . .'

'Forget all that romantic nonsense,' Carlos said roughly. 'If I paid you enough to buy your air ticket to England and some over, possibly enough to set up your own beauty salon ... would you agree to go through a civil marriage ceremony with me during the next few days, then drive with me to the ranch where I work and live there with me for a short while?'

'You must be crazy if you believe you can buy a wife!' Daphne exclaimed.

'I don't want to buy you,' he retorted exasperatedly.' I want to hire you to act the part of my wife for a while. You need a job and I need a wife, it's as simple as that. If you accept you would live in a fairly comfortable house and there wouldn't be any work for you to do. You would be better off than you were working for Elsa or if you managed to find a job in a beauty salon.'

'Act the part?' she repeated.' Does that mean you wouldn't expect me to be a proper wife? You wouldn't expect me to ... to ... make love with you?' She spoke quickly, her colour heightening.

'I wouldn't expect anything except your presence in my house and the right to introduce you to my mother and her relatives as my wife,' Carlos replied. 'The position would be a temporary one and would last only a few weeks, about a month. Then I would pay you and you could return to England and forget it ever happened. Are you interested?'

Daphne finished eating before replying.

'I'm intrigued,' she admitted at last. 'Why do you want a temporary wife?'

'If you agree to accept my offer you'll find out soon enough when we get to the ranch,' he replied grimly.

'Oh, really!' she exclaimed in irritation. 'How can I possibly accept your offer if you won't tell me why you need a wife in such a hurry?'

'I'll explain later, when you've agreed to marry me and not before,' he said smoothly.

'Couldn't you just hire me to pretend to be your wife without going through the civil ceremony?' she asked.

'I have to have legal proof that the marriage has taken place.'

'And what will you do if I refuse?'

He looked past her, his eyes narrowing, his mouth curling unpleasantly.

'Go on looking until I find another woman who is willing to put on an act provided she is paid enough,' he said tautly. 'It shouldn't be too hard to find someone in Mexico City who is willing to sell her services.' His glance focused on her again. 'But I would prefer to hire you. Your freshness and youth would make my marriage seem much more believable than any liaison with an older, more hardened woman would.'

Daphne gulped down the remains of the coffee in her mug.

'I suppose you think that because you helped me last night I'll accept your proposal,' she said.

'It had occurred to me that you might be the kind of person who would return one good turn with another,' he drawled mockingly.

'But I can't accept until I know more about you, more about your family,' she retorted stubbornly.

Giving her a glance that glittered with impatience, Carlos pushed back his chair and stood up.

'If you want to know more you'll have to come with me,' he replied coolly. 'If you're not interested you'll stay here and take your chances on finding a job on your own. I'm going to check out of the room now. I suggest you come and get your suitcase before I hand over the key, otherwise the management might think you're going to stay another night, and I'm sure you couldn't afford that.'

He turned and strode from the room. Daphne glanced at her watch. Five minutes to nine. Five minutes to make up her mind. What should she do? Go with him or stay here and hope to catch a bus back to Acapulco? On impulse she took a coin from her purse and tossed it up in the air. If it came down heads she would go with the enigmatic Carlos Reynolds. If it came down tails she would find out the time of the buses and catch one either to the capital or to Acapulco. The coin landed on the floor beside her chair and she bent to pick it up. It had landed heads up.

She put the coin in her purse and left the table to hurry through the entrance hall and up the stairway. Carlos was just walking out of the bedroom when she reached it.

'I . . . I'd like to come with you, please,' Daphne said breathlessly. 'But I must clean my teeth first.'

'Don't take too long,' he warned coolly. 'I'm not waiting for you.'

He was backing the car out of its parking slot in the quaint white-walled courtyard when she arrived lugging her suitcase. The sunshine was hot and the air was heavy and humid. Perspiration beaded Daphne's brow and soaked her cotton dress, making it limp as a rag. Seeing her, Carlos stopped the car. She opened the rear door, heaved her case on to the back seat and slammed the door shut. Then she opened the front door and slid into the front passenger seat. The tyres screeched as Carlos released the brakes and the car shot forward through an archway in the white wall on to a road which seemed to hang in the air above a deep valley, filled with trees. The car turned and Daphne gasped in appreciation of the panoramic view of mountains before them, ridges of bare rock glinting gold where the sun shone on them, glowing purple in the shadow. The road, blinding white in the sunlight, wound upwards to the crest of a hill, then seemed to disappear abruptly.

'Aren't we going back to the Highway?' asked Daphne after a few miles of hair-raising ride along the sinuous, dangerous road.

'No. This is the way to Taxco,' was the brief reply.

Hanging on to the strap attached to the door, glad that she had had the foresight to fasten her seat-belt, Daphne held her breath as the car topped yet another hill and then plunged down and up again, narrowly avoiding a car which was coming the other way.

She glanced sideways at her companion. Not only was he a man of few words, the strong silent type, she thought humorously, but he also had nerves of steel because he seemed quite un-perturbed by the steep, winding road and never slackened speed once.

Suddenly the tyres squealed as the brakes were applied sharply and the car came to a jolting stop, jerking her forward so that her forehead nearly hit the windscreen and she was thankful for the restraint of the seat-belt. Carlos let out some crisp expletives in English. Swerving round a bend, he had come across two bullocks ambling along the road. When they heard the screech of the car's brakes the animals stopped too, turning to stare. Greyish white in colour, they had black noses, soft slanting black eyes and up-curling, wicked-looking horns.

Carlos sounded the horn and opening the door leaned out to shout at the cattle in Spanish. They didn't move but continued to stare stupidly at the car. Slowly Carlos drove forward until the front of the car was almost touching the heaving flank of the nearest animal. At once it began to walk unhurriedly to the side of the road, its long tail swinging. The other animal followed and the car picked up speed.

'You said you work on the ranch,' Daphne said. 'What do you do?'

'I manage it for the owner, Claude Fontaine.'

'Like your father did?'

'*Si*.'

'What happened to your father?'

'He was killed, like yours, in an accident, about fifteen years ago. He was breaking in a horse. The horse threw him, and his neck was broken. Later my mother married again. She married Claude Fontaine.'

'My mother married again too,' Daphne went on, determined to dig more information out of him. 'I have two stepsisters. They're both older than I am and are married. Do you have any sisters or brothers?'

'Claude Fontaine had a daughter. I guess you could say she's my stepsister,' Carlos drawled indifferently.

'Older or younger than you?'

'Younger.'

'Married?'

'Married but getting a divorce,' he replied tersely.

'Is your mother expecting you to return to the ranch with a wife?' she persisted, refusing to be put off by his laconic answers.

'Maybe.'

'Maybe.' She mimicked the way he spoke, drawling out the words. 'What sort of answer is that?' she demanded irritably. 'Who do you think you are? Clint Eastwood?'

He gave her a surprised sidelong glance.

'Who is Clint Eastwood?' he asked.

'Oh, you're the limit!' she groaned. 'He's a film actor who's starred in some films about the American West and he never has much to say . . . like you. Don't you ever go to the movies?'

'I've been a few times, but not to see Westerns, and I know very little about film stars.'

'Then why were you at Elsa's party?'

'I was looking for a wife,' he drawled, and sent a wickedly mocking glance in her direction.

'Where did you meet Elsa?' she persisted.

'At a night club in Acapulco. She was sitting at the next table, and she came over and asked me to dance.'

Daphne took her glance off the view of mountains, heaps of rugged bare rock glittering against the brilliant sky, to stare at him. Yes, she could imagine her aunt being attracted by his stern hawkish profile, the paradox of the darkly tanned skin, black eyes and rough tawny brown hair. Elsa would have wanted to know more about him, and taking the initiative in her usual ostentatious way had asked him to dance with her instead of sitting and wishing he would ask her to dance with him.

'Were you alone at the night club?' she asked, imagining the scene, the dim lighting gleaming on the bare shoulders and arms of women, the rhythmic beat of guitars and drums, the clink of glasses, the hum of voices.

'I was.'

'Why did you go there?'

'For the same reason I went to Elsa's party—I was looking for a wife,' he drawled. 'Someone had told me that if I went to that particular club I might pick up an out-of-work actress who would be glad to earn a few bucks playing the part of my wife,' he added dryly.

'You should have asked Elsa,' she retorted acidly. 'I'm sure she would have jumped at the chance to be your wife.'

'She's too old and she happens to be married,' he replied coolly. 'Also I don't like the way she laughs.' He slanted her a glance. 'As I've said already, I find you much more suitable for the part.'

'I wish you'd tell me why you need a temporary wife,' she grumbled. 'It would be so much easier for me to agree to play the part if I knew why.'

'Marry me and you'll find out why,' he said curtly.

Defeated by his terse uninformative answers, Daphne slumped back in her seat and stared ahead. Huge spiky cacti grew by the roadside and beyond them the land fell away in rough ridges of rock to a wide valley where a river wound snakelike through thick green tropical vegetation.

'It's so wild up here and seems so far away from civilisation,' she commented.

'It isn't really as far as you think,' Carlos replied. 'We'll soon be in Taxco.'

'Why did you come this way? Why didn't you take the toll road to Mexico City?'

'We would have reached the capital too quickly and I'm trying to give you time to make up your mind. Also I'm still on vacation and I've never been to Taxco. That was why I was in Acapulco, to have a holiday.'

'Oh. I thought you were there to find a wife,' Daphne taunted, and looked round at him to see how he reacted. His slow grin creased the cheek, she could see, attractively.

'That too,' he remarked briefly.

Daphne leaned back again. The road snaked around another bend and she could see a town on a hillside, a jumble of redtiled roofs towered over by a big church built of glowing pink stone. But she wasn't really interested in it, she was too taken up by her confused thoughts. Part of her, the practical, down-to-earth part, rejected outright Carlos Reynolds' suggestion that she should be his wife for a short time. Even though he had offered to pay her the whole idea struck her as being crazy in the extreme as well as full of pitfalls and dangers. How could she possibly go through a legal ceremony of marriage with a complete stranger and then pretend to be his wife in front of his relatives?

Daphne shook her head negatively so that the thick wave of hair across her forehead shimmered with golden lights. Makebelieve, pretending to be what she wasn't, had never appealed to her. Elsa was the only actress the Thomas family had produced and Daphne had never had any desire to imitate her aunt. For her life had to be real, not an illusion, not something that had to be acted out in front of an audience. For her marriage would have to be real too. She could only marry a man she had chosen because she admired and respected him, and once married to him she would be a proper wife, an active partner in a relationship which would grow and develop over the years. She couldn't possibly pretend to be a wife.

And yet part of her, the other imaginative, adventurous and generous part was intrigued by the suggestion. Only if she agreed to marry Carlos would her lively curiosity as to why he needed a temporary wife be satisfied because it was obvious he would never tell her why. If she agreed to marry him she would be taken to another part of this beautiful, exciting country, would learn something about a different way of life and meet people she would never meet otherwise. And above all if she married him she would be helping someone, something which appealed to her warm, affectionate nature.

Helping whom? Carlos Reynolds? Her glance slid away from the highway which was now climbing through the outskirts of the town to the profile of the man at her side. Looking at his proud self-contained face, she couldn't believe that he would ever need help to do anything and judging by the way he behaved he seemed like a man who was fully in control of his own life, knew exactly where he was going and how to get there. Certainly he didn't seem the sort of person who would need the help of someone like herself.

But how could his marriage, a brief temporary marriage at that, help anyone else? She longed to know and the only way she could find out was to marry him and masquerade as his wife for a while; live in his house, go places with him. And in return she would be paid enough money to pay her fare to Britain and more, sufficient to set up her own business. Of course she could do it.

The argument between her two selves was still going on when the car turned off the highway at a corner by a petrol station and swung up a narrow cobblestoned street, past white-walled buildings and wrought iron gateways, turning at the top into a *zocalo*, the central square. In the middle of the square was an old bandstand and around it were benches set under shady trees. Carlos parked the car among some others near to the overpowering, ornately-decorated pink church, switched off the engine and turned to her.

'So here we are in the Silver City,' he remarked.

'Why is it called that?' she asked.

'Back in the eighteenth century a Frenchman called José de la Borda discovered one of the richest veins of silver ever found in the country. It's supposed to have produced forty million *pesos* of silver. Now Taxco is known for its silversmiths who create many beautiful silver ornaments and jewellery and sell them. Would you like to get out and walk around for a while? We could have lunch here. After all, you and I might never come this way again, so we should see all we can while we can.' He smiled at her, a slightly crooked but attractive curving of his lips.

Her heart seemed to swell in her breast and she felt suddenly giddy, and for some reason she couldn't look away from the gaze of the black eyes which were softened now by the coming together of the thick short black lashes as he smiled. She felt she had been caught up in a magic spell; as if she were taking part in a fairy tale in which anything could happen. Or was she dreaming that she was there in the quaint old colonial town with its narrow twisting streets, high balconied windows hinting at romance, being invited by a handsome mysterious stranger to go exploring with him.

Daphne pinched her thigh stealthily. Nothing changed. She didn't wake up and find herself back at Elsa's house or in the bedroom of the hotel near Iguala. And the pink church with its richly carved doorways and towers was really there, although it seemed to be shimmering before her eyes as waves of heat rose around it.

'*Que pasa?* What's wrong? Do you feel ill?'

His hand, its palm hard and dry and a little rough, covered one of hers and held it strongly. He leaned towards her, so near that she could see a reflection of herself very tiny and far off in the depths of his eyes.

'No . . . at . . . least . . . I feel a little dizzy, that's all,' she whispered, raising her other hand and pushing the hair back from her brow.

'It's the change in altitude, I expect,' he said practically, still holding her hand, looking into her eyes as if he too were spellbound.' This city is five thousand feet above sea-level and its atmosphere is much rarer than Acapulco's or Iguala's, although not as rare as the capital's. We made the ascent too fast for you, perhaps. I had forgotten you are not accustomed to the changes. We'll sit here for a while until you feel better.'

'Thank you. I . . . I'm sure I'll be all right in a few minutes,' she muttered, looking away down at the hand covering hers—skin tanned to the colour of golden hide, long sinewy fingers, a hand that had worked most of its life. She liked it and had no objections to it touching hers. In fact she would have no objection to it touching her anywhere.

Daphne's errant thoughts braked sharply. Shocked by the direction in which they had wandered, she pulled her hand from beneath his and picking up her handbag from the floor of the car slung it over her shoulder.

'I'm all right now,' she said with false cheerfulness. 'Do you think we can go into the church? It looks very interesting.'

'We can go anywhere you like.'

For the next hour they wandered about, doing everything that tourists do, lingering for a few moments in the gold-bright church, visiting the museum behind it to view the Spratling collection of Pre-Columban silver ornaments, walking down steep streets, too narrow and rough for cars, which were surfaced with loose grey and pink stones, calling in at some of the small shops to admire the work of modern silversmiths. In a small restaurant they lunched on *tacos de pollo*, which were *tortillas* rolled into tubes with fillings of shredded fried chicken served with sour cream, fried beans and onions, and drank *café con leche*. After the meal they walked back to the *zócalo*.

Carlos was unlocking the door of the car when the policeman approached him. Wearing a blue uniform, dark trousers with a lighter shirt, the man held a notebook in his hand which he consulted as he asked Carlos a question. Carlos nodded and from the inside of his jacket produced a wallet and showed something to the policeman. Daphne guessed he was showing some form of identification.

The policeman looked across at her and asked her a question. Not understanding him, she looked appealingly at Carlos.

'He wants to see your identification,' said Carlos. 'Show him your passport.'

Daphne took her passport from her handbag and handed it to the policeman. He opened it, studied it for a moment then consulted with Carlos about it. He handed it back to Daphne and said something else to Carlos, who frowned and answered sharply. The policeman got angry and waved his hands about.

'What's the matter? What's he saying?' demanded Daphne, sensing that something was wrong by the way passersby were stopping to stand and stare at the policeman.

'He is insisting that we accompany him to the police department to be questioned by his superior officer who can speak English,' said Carlos.

'Why? Is there something wrong with my passport?' Daphne asked anxiously.

Carlos translated her question for the benefit of the policeman, who shook his head negatively and explained at length in Spanish why he wanted them to go with him.

'All he says is that his superior wants to talk to us, so I guess we'd better go along with him,' said Carlos, shrugging his shoulders. 'Come on. It's in a building not far from here and I guess the inquisition won't take too long. You and I have nothing to hide and once he knows the truth about us he'll let us go.'

The police department was in a low white building on a street near the *zócalo* and they were shown by the policeman into a plain room furnished with a desk and some chairs. Behind the desk sat a slim brown-skinned man who was wearing a slightly different uniform from the policeman. He rose to his feet courteously when they entered and indicated that they should sit in the chairs which the policeman brought forward for them.

'I am Captain Delaguerra,' he explained in English when they were all sitting down. 'Sergeant Sotomayor has examined your identification and is satisfied that you are the two people we have been asked to bring in.'

'Bring in?' Daphne couldn't help exclaiming. 'But why?—what have we done?'

The Captain glanced at her, a slight frown creasing his high brown forehead.

'Sergeant Sotomayor has assured me that you are Miss Daphne Thomas, the niece of Miss Elsa Thomas, the film star, who is presently residing in Acapulco,' he said.

'That's right, I am related to Elsa Thomas. Has something happened to her? Is that why you want to see me?'

'No, no.' The Captain spoke hastily. 'Nothing has happened to Miss Elsa Thomas. But she believes that something unpleasant has happened to you and she has asked that a warrant be put out for the arrest of this man here.'

'She wants me arrested?' Carlos exclaimed, then laughed. 'Why, for God's sake? What have I done?'

'Miss Elsa Thomas believes you have kidnapped her only niece Miss Daphne Thomas and have carried her off against her will. She knew that you, *señor*, were driving to Mexico City when you left Acapulco because you had told her when you left her house, and she asked for the police of the towns along the way to keep a lookout for you. The message was passed on by the police to innkeepers and motel proprietors. Last night at an inn near Iguala the night clerk was suspicious of you and when he went off duty this morning he informed the police in Iguala about you. By the time they reached the inn this morning you had left, saying you intended to come to Taxco.

We were informed. Sergeant Sotomayor recognised your car in the square and waited there for
your return and then brought you here.' Captain
Delaguerra paused, looking very stern. 'And now
it is my duty to charge you with kidnapping Miss
Daphne Thomas and to detain you in prison until
you are brought to trial.'

Carlos said something in Spanish, slowly yet
with unmistakable viciousness. Daphne guessed
he had been rude by the reaction of the police
captain, who stiffened and rapped out something
in the same language. The police sergeant moved
forward, unclipping a set of handcuffs from his
belt.

'Oh, no!' Daphne leapt to her feet. 'What are
you going to do?' she exclaimed. 'You can't put
him in prison. It's unjust! He hasn't done anything wrong or criminal.' She turned urgently
towards the police captain, aware that the sergeant
had forced Carlos to get to his feet and was hand-
cuffing his wrists together behind his back. 'Oh,
please listen to me,' she cried. 'Carlos didn't
kidnap me—I'm travelling with him willingly.
We're going to Mexico City. Surely I should
know if he's kidnapped me or not? Wouldn't I be
glad to be here, if he had? Wouldn't I be glad
that you're going to imprison him if he'd carried
me away against my will?'

Captain Delaguerra stared at her across the
width of his desk, his lean brown face impassive,
his dark brown eyes unwinking.

'Your aunt, Miss Elsa Thomas, informed the
police in Acapulco last night that her husband,

Mr Mitchell Gardner, saw this man push you into his car and drive off at full speed. Mr Gardner said he tried to prevent the kidnapping but that Reynolds got hold of him and threw him aside.'

'Oh, what a lot of lies!' exclaimed Daphne, her quick temper boiling up. 'Mr Gardner did nothing of the sort. He was assaulting me and I really believe he would have raped me, if Mr Reynolds hadn't come along and rescued me. I was glad to get into the car and be driven away, and I wasn't pushed into it, I got into it of my own free will.'

Captain Delaguerra leaned back in his chair and studied her with narrowed eyes.

'So what about last night?' he said softly. 'Did you stay with him at the inn near Iguala as his wife of your own free will? The night clerk reported that you seemed disturbed—that is why he was suspicious.'

'Yes, I did stay with Mr Reynolds as his wife of my own free will,' Daphne replied sturdily, never blinking an eyelid.

There was a short tense silence while Daphne and Captain Delaguerra measured glances. A fly buzzed against a windowpane. The old-fashioned fan attached to the ceiling made a clanking sound as it went round and round, wafting the warm air about and giving an impression of coolness only. For Daphne they were the most difficult moments of her life. She could feel her cheeks burning and hear her heart pounding. Sweat began to break out on her brow. Suddenly Captain Delaguerra's glance shifted. He looked past her to Carlos.

'Why are you going to Mexico City?' he snapped.

'To be married there, to Daphne,' was the cool answer. 'Then we shall go on to the ranch where I live and work in the state of Veracruz.'

'Is it true, what he says?' The captain's sharp glance returned to Daphne. 'Are you going to marry him?'

Daphne glanced sideways at Carlos, thoughts racing through her head. She could see he was furious, inwardly blazing with anger in spite of his outward cool poise, and she guessed he was resenting having had his freedom taken away from him. If she didn't go along with what he had said and say she was going to marry him he would be locked up in a cell to await trial on an unjust charge. She couldn't let that happen to him. She couldn't let Elsa and Mitchell do that to him.

'Yes, it's true. We are going to be married,' she said, turning appealing to the captain. 'My aunt . . . Elsa Thomas doesn't approve,' she went on, amazed at her own ability to invent on the spur of the moment, 'so we decided to go away together to the capital to be married. Aunt Elsa found out we were leaving and she sent her husband to stop us and. . . .'

'Then you are eloping?' The captain snapped the question at her.

'No, no,' she denied. 'Oh, you can call it that if you like, but I don't. I'm twenty-two and I don't need anyone's consent to marry. Aunt Elsa has no right to interfere in my life, no right at all. She isn't my guardian. I'm a free woman; free to

choose my own husband. Now please will you take
those dreadful things off Carlos's wrists and let
us go on our way. We would like to be married as
soon as possible—we've waited too long as it is.
Now do you still believe that Carlos has kidnapped me?'

The thin brown face didn't soften. The dark
brown eyes continued to stare at her.

'This could be a trick,' he said.

'What do you mean?' she demanded, angry
again.

'You could be lying about going to be married
to him.' Thin lips curled into a cruel sneer. 'Why
should I believe you? What proof have you that
you are going to be married?'

Behind her Daphne heard Carlos swear in
Spanish. At once the captain reprimanded him in
the same language. Carlos answered him again
and there was a short exchange of words between
them that Daphne couldn't understand. At last
Carlos turned to her and said,

'He will only believe we are going to be married
if we go through the ceremony here and now.'

'And if we don't?'

'He will put us both in jail to wait until your
aunt comes.'

'Oh no, I'm not going to jail, and I'm not waiting for Aunt Elsa either,' said Daphne spiritedly.

'So?' Carlos's eyes challenged her across the
room. She was trapped, she thought ruefully, in a
corner from which there was only one way to
escape, and she hesitated only briefly before
taking that way.

'So we'll be married here, today, if that's possible,' she replied.

'And you'll go through with the rest?' Carlos queried softly.

'Yes, I'll go through with the rest,' she said.

'*Muchas gracias, querida,*' he said, triumph flickering for a moment in his eyes. 'If it wasn't for these damned handcuffs I would show you how much I appreciate your agreement to marry me here, this afternoon.' He turned to the captain and said, 'Are you satisfied now that we are speaking the truth, that I didn't kidnap her and that we intend to get married?'

'I am satisfied,' said Captain Delaguerra, rising to his feet. He gave instruction to the sergeant to unlock the handcuffs. At once Carlos stepped across to Daphne and taking hold of her shoulders drew her towards him. Bending his head, he kissed her on the lips.

Amazingly her lips responded to the touch of his, parting slightly under pressure. She felt his mouth move against her mouth and experienced a strange upsurge of excitement, a desire to prolong the kiss and to find out where it would lead her. But the caress was only for the benefit of the watching policeman. It was all part of the crazy masquerade in which she had become involved, and it ended as swiftly as it had begun. Carlos raised his head, stared down at her for a moment with cold calculating eyes, then releasing her turned away to speak to the police captain.

A few minutes later they left the office and, escorted by Captain Delaguerra and Sergeant

Sotomayor, they walked to another building and in another office they applied formally to be married. The quick civil ceremony took place two hours later in the same office with the two police-men acting as witnesses. Only then were they allowed to leave Taxco and drive on to Cuernavaca to stay the night. In Carlos's jacket pocket there was the document which proved they were husband and wife.

CHAPTER THREE

PASTURELAND, flat and seemingly limitless, extended on either side of the highway, its mono-tony broken only here and there by clusters of banana plantations. In the far distance Daphne thought she could just see the shapes of hills and beyond them the peaks of mountains, hazy blue shapes against a sky streaked with sunset colours.

She shifted in her seat. She felt sticky and hot even though the sun was going down. They had been travelling all day with only two stops, one in Mexico City, the other in Tuxpan, a small but clean and pleasant port on the Gulf of Mexico. From there they had driven south and had turned inland along this highway which followed a river valley. The only place of interest since Tuxpan had been the small cattle market town of Micatepec, where the older buildings had shown the influence of France rather than of Spain.

Soon they would arrive at the Fontaine ranch and she would be meeting Carlos' mother and other relatives. She would be introduced to them as his wife. Señora Carlos Reynolds. Daphne moved uneasily in her seat again. Would she ever be able to relate to that title? She was still having difficulty in believing that the quick businesslike ceremony which had taken place in Taxco had changed her name and status and had provided Carlos with the proof that he required that he was legally married.

She glanced sideways at Carlos. Silent and composed, seemingly completely relaxed as he drove the car, one hand only on the steering wheel, his other arm draped casually along the top of the back of the long front seat, he wasn't any different from what he had been before he had married her. In Cuernavaca where they had stayed the previous night they had again shared a bedroom, but not a bed because there had been two beds in the hotel room and Carlos had kept his distance. Apart from the kiss he had given her in the office of the police captain in Taxco he had kept strictly to his side of their bargain. He hadn't touched her, he hadn't attempted to make love to her. He hadn't told her why he needed a temporary wife, either.

Daphne sighed involuntarily and he turned his head to glance at her.

'Are you tired?' he asked.

'A little. We've driven a long way. Do we have much further to go?'

'No. In about fifteen minutes we'll be on Fontaine land. We'll turn in through a gate in this fence on the left of the road and take the dirt road to the ranch house.'

'I wish I knew more about the ranch and about your mother and stepsister,' she said. 'I don't even know their names.'

Carlos gave her another sidelong glance and frowned.

'Okay,' he drawled. 'As soon as we're off the road I'll brief you, give you some information about them.'

'Thank you.'

A few miles farther on they reached the gate he had mentioned and he turned the car towards it. Leaving the car's engine running, he got out, swung the gate open, returned to the car, drove it through the opening, then got out again to go back and close the gate.

When he returned to the car he switched off the engine. Silence enfolded them. Grassland, tawny gold under the rays of the setting sun, stretched away into purple shadows which were gathering along the distant horizon. There were no buildings in sight and the only signs of life were some cattle grazing, the same sort they had passed on the road near Taxco, with greyish white hides and black noses.

'I've never seen cattle like them before,' said Daphne.

'They're *zebu*, imported Asian beasts. This is a prize herd.' There was a certain pride in the way he told her, 'The land as far as you can see it belongs to the Fontaine ranch. Years ago it was a much bigger *hacienda*. My stepfather inherited the property from his father, who in turn inherited it from his and so on, right back to about 1830 when the first Fontaine came over from France with other immigrants. They belonged to the old landholding class which held all the political power in Mexico until the Revolution.'

'When was the Revolution?' asked Daphne.

'At the beginning of this century. After the Revolution the land was redistributed and the landowners lost their power. The Fontaines were left with about eight hundred acres of the original *hacienda*.'

'What happened to the rest of the land?'

'It was granted to Mexicans who had always lived and worked on it. You see, under the old system nine Mexicans out of ten were held in virtual slavery on the big estates. For the owners of the estates life was a thing of graciousness and luxury and most of the time they weren't there. They were living it up in the capitals and resorts of Europe. But the peasants lived lives of utter poverty. My mother's father was one of the slaves until he joined the Zapatistas.'

'Who were they?'

'Followers of Emiliano Zapata, who led the revolt. The Zapatistas, unlike the other revolutionaries, were interested only in getting back the land which they believed belonged to them. They would burn down *hacienda* buildings, claim the land, then divide it up among them and turn from soldiering to farming.'

'Did your grandfather burn the buildings on the Fontaine *hacienda*?' she asked, fascinated by the brief history he was giving her of the country.

'No. The Fontaine of the time was shrewd enough to hand over some of the land if they spared his house and cattle. That land was formed into *ejidos*, village-owned communal farms. My mother grew up in one of the villages near here. She used to work as a housemaid for the Fontaines. That was how she met my father when he came here to manage the ranch.'

'And also how she met your stepfather, too, I suppose. When did she marry Claude Fontaine?'

'About five years after my father was killed.'

'Did you object when she remarried?' Daphne asked.

'No. Why should I? I wasn't around at the time. Soon after my father was killed I left Mexico and went to the States to work on ranches in Texas and New Mexico, to learn my trade.'

'How long were you away?'

'I came back six years ago. Claude had become ill, and the ranch had deteriorated through lack of good management. At my mother's suggestion he asked me to manage it for him. He died a few months ago.'

'I suppose your stepsister inherited the ranch,' she commented.

'The terms of his will haven't been carried out yet,' Carlos replied coolly, and turning on the car's engine eased it into gear. Slowly the vehicle lurched forward over the rough sun-baked surface of the road. 'My stepsister is called Ana-Maria and my mother's name is Teresa,' he added casually. 'Is there anything else you think you should know?'

'Yes. Isn't your mother going to think it strange when you arrive with a woman you've never mentioned and introduce her as your wife?'

'What makes you think I've never mentioned you to my mother?' he asked.

'How could you have told her about me when you didn't know me until two days ago?'

'My mother knows I met a woman in Acapulco last year. You are that woman,' he said blandly.

'But how can I be? My name must be different from hers,' Daphne exclaimed, turning to stare at him.

'True,' he conceded easily. 'But I never told my mother the name of the other woman—the one I went to Acapulco to marry.'

'Why didn't you marry her?' she challenged him.

'I couldn't find her,' he replied, 'so I had to search for someone else to be my wife.'

'Oh, I don't understand you,' she raged, annoyed with his secretiveness.

'You don't have to. Understanding and emotional involvement aren't part of the deal we made,' he retorted coldly. 'There's to be no romance. You have to do only what I ask you for a while and you'll be paid and released from the arrangement in a few weeks' time.'

'But supposing your mother asks me questions about myself, where I come from and so on. What shall I tell her?

'Tell her the truth about working for Elsa. The only lie you'll have to tell her concerns the time. You're the woman I met in Acapulco last year and went there to marry this year.'

'Oh, all right,' she muttered. 'But you're asking an awful lot.'

'I'll be paying for it,' Carlos reminded her acidly.

Biting her lip, Daphne looked away out of the window. Flat and desolate as darkness crept across it, the scenery was completely alien to her, and she longed suddenly to be among the mountains of Wales. Was it because she was tired that she felt suddenly forlorn. The spirit of adventure which had carried her through the marriage ceremony and had brought her all this way today had evaporated, and she wished suddenly that she had run away from Carlos in Cuernavaco. There had been plenty of opportunity. He hadn't locked her up or prevented her freedom of movement. Or she could have escaped from him in the teeming, polluted, magnificent capital of Mexico, disappeared into the crowds.

But she hadn't taken those opportunities. She had stayed with him. Why? Because she had given him her word in Taxco that she would do as he asked—be his masquerade wife for as long as he wanted in return for her air-ticket to London and some over, and she had never gone back on a promise yet.

The sun had slid behind the line of distant hills and the light was fading fast from the sky when she saw the ranch buildings at last, the old-fashioned French tiles of the roofs of the house, barns and stable gleaming softly grey in the short tropical twilight. Set slightly apart from the group of buildings were two other buildings, low and modern in design, one long with several windows, the other square in shape with a shady verandah over its front windows and door. It was to that building that Carlos drove and stopped the car in front of it.

Daphne opened the car door and stepped out. Her head was aching and she longed for nothing more than a bath and a comfortable bed where she could sleep and sleep and sleep. As she walked round to the back of the car to take her case from the boot which Carlos was unlocking, the door of the long building opened and light streamed out across a yard of hard-packed earth. A man shouted something in Spanish and Carlos shouted back in the same language. The man answered, his voice rising in surprise and pleasure. He jumped down the few steps which led up to the door and walked across the yard.

'This is José Valdez, a cousin of mine and the ranch foreman,' Carlos explained in a low voice to Daphne as he closed the boot. 'He can speak some English. I'll tell him who you are. Try and say something to him in his language, if you can.'

The man was short and wide-shouldered. His features were broad and of a definite Indian cast. His hair was coarse and black and he was wearing a loose white collarless shirt, narrow grey pants with a dark stripe down the outside of each leg and leather riding boots. Carlos introduced her and the man's teeth flashed in a smile against his swarthy skin. He slapped Carlos on the back and said in heavily accented English,

'So you do it at last, *amigo*. I am glad.' He turned to Daphne. 'You are welcome, *señora*.'

'*Muchas gracias, señor,*' said Daphne, and added a little self consciously, stumbling over the pronunciation, '*Mucho gusto en conocerle*. I'm pleased to meet you.'

'*El gusto es mio*. The pleasure is mine,' he replied gallantly, bowing slightly from the hips. He picked up her case and together they followed Carlos up the steps of the verandah and into the bungalow.

Accustomed as she had been for the past six months to luxurious surroundings, Daphne found the inside of the bungalow plain and shabby. The floor of the living room into which Carlos led her was uncarpeted, the walls were rough and painted plain white and the furniture was very simple. There were several bamboo armchairs with cushioned seats, a low table in front of the window, a roll-topped desk against one wall and an old-fashioned sideboard against another.

After putting her case down José left the room. Carlos went with him to the front door and she could hear them talking in low voices. Then the door was closed, and Carlos came back back into the room.

'We'll clean up, have a wash and change our clothes and then go over to the house. I'd like you to meet my mother and my stepsister as soon as possible.'

'Couldn't I meet them tomorrow?' asked Daphne, one hand to her head. 'I can't meet them tonight—I don't feel like it. I have a headache.'

He had turned away to pick up her suitcase, but on hearing her complaint he swung round to face her again, his mouth twisting sardonically.

'The usual wifely complaint?' he drawled tauntingly. 'Then take something for it. I suppose you have some aspirins.'

'No, I haven't. Anyway, aspirins wouldn't make any difference. I'll have to go to bed, lie down. The drive was too long—I'm not used to riding in a car for such long distances. I'll meet your mother and stepsister in the morning.'

'No, not tomorrow. Now, tonight,' he said firmly, stepping over to her, standing close to her, his hands on his hips.

The blue shirt he was wearing was open almost to the waist, unbuttoned for coolness during the heat of the day, revealing the rough dark hairs on his chest. Sweat gleamed in the hollow at the base of his sun-bronzed throat. She was suddenly aware of his masculinity in a way that hadn't happened to her before. Strange sensations pricked inside her. She wanted to step closer to him, lean against him, rest her aching head against his broad chest, slide her hand within his shirt to feel his heartbeat, hoping that his arms would go round her in comfort and that his lips would take hers in desire.

She stepped back sharply, alarmed by what was happening to her. With one hand she pushed back the thick hair from her hot brow. The blood was boiling beneath the thin skin of her wrists and temples.

'I'm too tired to cope with your family tonight,' she whispered. 'If . . . if you were a proper husband you would understand and be more considerate of the way I feel.'

'I want you to meet them while I'm around,' Carlos said flatly, his lips thinning. 'Tomorrow morning won't do because I'll be up early, long before you, to go out on the range to find out what has been happening while I've been away.' His eyes narrowed. 'As for me being a proper husband, I have to remind you that I hired you to play the part of being my wife only and I have no intention of making the relationship real or lasting. Now I'll show you where the bedroom is. There's a bathroom near it. You can wash and change, and put on a decent dress.' His hard glance raked her critically from head to foot. 'I'm sure you can make yourself look better than you look right now.'

'No!' she flung at him defiantly, her cheeks flaming in reaction to his criticism. 'I don't see why I should do what you say. You can't make me wash and change my clothes if I don't want to.'

'I can—very easily,' he threatened softly, stepping closer to her.

'What are you going to do?' She backed away nervously and he followed.

'You're behaving like a child, so I'll treat you like a child. I'll wash your face, comb your hair, change your clothes for you and then take you with me to meet my mother.'

'Don't you dare touch me!' she muttered through gritted teeth, forgetting that only seconds ago she had been longing for him to take her in his arms and kiss her.

The black eyes glinted suddenly with wicked humour and he shook his head from side to side at the same time, clucking his tongue against his teeth to mock her.

'You should never say that to me,' he drawled, 'because I'll dare to do anything.'

In one stride he closed in on her and scooped her up in his arms.

'Put me down!' raged Daphne, striking at him with her fists, feeling extremely helpless.

'Not until we're in the bathroom.'

Carlos set her down just inside the door of the small room, kicked the door closed and moving round her turned on the taps of the bath.

'Now are you going to take off your clothes or am I?' he threatened silkily, stepping over to her again, his hand reaching towards the opening of her blouse.

'No! Oh, all right, I'll do as you say.' She gave in suddenly, glaring up at him, her eyes glittering with unshed tears, one hand at her breast holding the opening of her blouse protectively. 'If . . . If . . . I'd known you could be so . . . so . . . cruel I wouldn't have agreed to marry you in Taxco. I'd have let them put you in jail and you could have rotted there!'

His face went stiff and his black eyes gleamed murder at her for a moment, but he said nothing

and opening the door left the room. The door
closed behind him. Hands pressed against her
throbbing temples, Daphne glared at it while tears
slid down her cheeks—tears of anger and frustration; anger with herself for having so foolishly
agreed to marry a stranger; frustration because she
had lost her first battle with Carlos since she had
agreed to be his wife.

Realising the taps were still running, she turned
them off, then, undressing, she stepped into the
bath. Tepid water closed over her hot sticky body
as she lay down, bringing a certain amount of re-
lease from tension.

The bath was long and narrow with high sides.
She looked round the room. The ceiling and walls
were painted white and had become discoloured.
In places the paint was peeling off. Her nose
wrinkled in distaste. It wasn't a very attractive
house. She had expected much better for the
manager of a big ranch. She had always assumed
ranchers to be very wealthy for some reason. Oh,
well, she wouldn't be here for long. About a
month, Carlos had said.

The bathroom door opened again and he strode
in. Hands on his hips, he looked down at her.

'You've been in long enough. Get out,' he
ordered crisply. 'There's only one bathroom and
I would like to wash too.'

Sitting up suddenly so that the water swirled
around her, covering her breasts with her arms to
hide them from his curious gaze, Daphne glared
at him furiously.

'I'll get out of the bath only when you get out

of this room,' she snapped. 'You've no right to come in here when I'm bathing!'

He gave her one of his most sardonic glances, turned away and whisked a rough wide towel from the towel rack and tossed it to her. She managed to catch it before it fell into the water.

'The bedroom is the next door along the passage,' he said as he strode towards the doorway. 'You'll find your suitcase in there.'

The door closed again. Still angry, Daphne got out of the bath, draped the towel about her sarong-wise and gathering up her discarded clothing left the room to hurry along a dark passage to a doorway through which light slanted out.

The bedroom was square and furnished with one wide bed covered with an Indian blanket woven in bright colours. A big chest of drawers made from shiny red mahogany stood against one wall. Over it was an oval mirror. On top of the chest was a man's hairbrush, a comb, a long narrow wooden box and a framed photograph.

With water still dripping from her wet body Daphne leaned forward to peer closely at the photograph. There were three people in it, a man a woman and a boy. The man was tall and lean and had a lot of straw-coloured hair. His face was tough, long-jawed and beaky-nosed. He was wearing a checked shirt, close-fitting denim levis and short leather riding boots. His right arm was round the shoulders of the woman. His left arm hung at his side and there was a white stetson in his left hand.

The woman was short and rather plump. Her black hair was drawn back from her round smiling face into a knot at the nape of her neck. Her skin was dusky gold in colour and her teeth were very large and white. She was wearing a simple white blouse and a full dark skirt.

It was easy to guess that the boy was Carlos at about the age of ten, dressed exactly like his father in checked shirt, levis and riding boots, his hair lighter than it was now. He was smiling too, obviously pleased to be having his photograph taken. It was a simple family group, the sort that could be found in any home, not unlike a photograph Daphne possessed of her own parents and herself. A happily married couple with their child. For some reason Daphne felt a lump rise in her throat.

'*Dios mio*, aren't you dressed yet?'

Carlos spoke immediately behind her and she turned quickly, startled. He had come into the room and like her was wearing only a towel. It was draped round his hips and the suntanned skin of his wide shoulders gleamed under the electric light. She found it hard to associate his tough adult muscularity with the little boy in the photograph and could find no sign of the boy's round cheeks and impish grin in the lean sardonic face.

'I can't get dressed now that you're in the room,' she retorted, watching him open a drawer in the chest and take out some underwear. Quickly she turned away and went over to her suitcase which he had placed on the bed. 'I didn't think we'd have to share a bedroom here,' she complained as she clicked undone the fastenings of the case. 'Aren't there two bedrooms?'

'No.'

'Did your parents live in this house when your father was manager of the ranch?'

'*Si*. Claude had it built for them.'

'Then where did you sleep?' she asked.

'At first, in here, in a cot. Later when I was older, in the loft, under the roof.'

'Well, couldn't you sleep in the loft while I'm here?' she asked. She had found a dress. Made of thin silky material patterned with flowers, it had full long sleeves and a gathered skirt, and it wasn't creased.

'I could, I guess,' Carlos drawled, 'but the loft is crammed full of things. If you really want to sleep in here alone you could tidy the loft tomorrow, it would give you something to do. Hey, where are you going?'

He snapped the question at her sharply and she turned in the doorway, her dress and fresh underwear clutched in her arms.

'To the bathroom to get dressed!' she hissed furiously, and banged the door shut.

Carlos was in the living room waiting for her when she went in there. Lean and lithe in close-fitting grey trousers like José Valdez had been wearing, and a loose white cotton shirt, he came towards her, his glance flicking over her critically again.

'Are you ready to go now?' he asked.

'I'm ready,' she said stiffly. While she had been dressing she had come to terms with herself and this job Carlos had hired her to do. It was a job and that was all, and she must keep it in mind and not let her emotions get involved. She must always try to keep her cool and never lose her temper with him. She must never let him get beneath her skin, because once that happened she would be lost.

'Is your headache better?' Was it her imagination or was there an unkind taunt in the drawling voice suggesting that he had never believed she had had a headache.

'Almost,' she replied curtly. She must ignore his taunts. She mustn't let him hurt her. Or at least, she mustn't let him see she could be hurt by anything he said.

'I like the dress,' he said, coming closer, bending his head to look into her eyes. 'Blue makes your eyes look bluer.' He raised a hand and stroked a knuckle down her cheeks. 'I suppose you know you're pretty, with your peaches and cream complexion, your golden hair and blue eyes—typically English.'

'Welsh,' she croaked, correcting him, her voice shaking, and her lashes swept down to cover her eyes in case they were expressing her confusion at this new approach of his.

'Welsh, then. *No importa*,' he shrugged. 'My mother won't know any differently. You will just come under the heading of *gringo*, for her.'

'What does it mean?' she asked.

'It's a word Mexicans use to refer to anyone who is not Mexican. Some foreigners have made the mistake of thinking it is a word of abuse, but it isn't. It derives from the Spanish *griego*, meaning Greek.'

'Will she mind that you've married a *gringo*?' Daphne asked.

'She married one herself, so why should she?' Carlos retorted easily. 'Let's go now.'

Outside it was very dark in spite of the stars in the sky, and she was glad he was there to guide her across the yard, past the windmill and the stable to the ranchhouse. The air was slightly cooler and a breeze rustled the long grasses. Strips of yellow light glimmered from between the slats of wooden shutters which had been closed over the lower windows of the old house and two lamps shaped like lanterns gleamed on either side of the tall intricately-carved wooden front doors which stood open giving access to a wide porch with a tiled floor.

Carlos opened the inner door, which was half glass decorated with trailing vine leaves and bunches of grapes and Daphne stepped past him into a dimly lit cool hallway. It was like stepping into another world, into the faded elegance of the nineteenth century. A woman came out of a doorway on the right. She was the woman of the photograph, much older now, her black hair liberally sprinkled with grey, her golden-brown face thinner and lined, wrinkles crinkling around her black eyes as she smiled and approached Carlos with her arms outstretched affectionately.

She kissed him on both cheeks, then spoke to him in rapid Spanish. He answered her and taking her arm turned her about to face Daphne.

'Mother, this is my wife Daphne. We were married yesterday in Taxco. She doesn't understand our language yet, so please speak to her in English. Daphne, this is my mother, Teresa Fontaine.' He made the introduction politely but without bothering to give all his mother's last names in the usual Mexican fashion, for which Daphne was glad because she would have only found them confusing.

Teresa Fontaine was staring at her with rounded surprised black eyes and was apparently struck dumb by Carlos' announcement. Making a supreme effort, Daphne forced her lips into a smile and held out her hand.

'*Buenas noches, señora*, I'm pleased to meet you,' she said.

'You are welcome,' Teresa replied huskily, taking Daphne's hand in both of hers. She spoke English like Carlos did, with a slight drawl. 'I hope you will be happy in your marriage to my son.'

She turned to say something to Carlos, but broke off as feet sounded on the stairway. A young woman was running down the stairs, her thick shoulder-length reddish-brown hair flying out behind her. She ran up to Carlos, her arms stretched out.

'Carlos, *mucho gusto en verle!*' she exclaimed.

She went right up to him and he took both her hands in his and held her away from him when she would have flung her arms about him.

'When did you come back?' he asked in English.

'Two days ago. I came just in time, you see, but find you not here. But now at last you come and at last we can do what my father wished.' The young woman, who was small and slim, spoke English with a strong lisping accent. 'But why are we speaking English?' she demanded.

'For the benefit of my wife, Daphne.' Carlos let go of the woman's hands and stepping to Daphne's side put his arm about her shoulders and smiled down at her.' Daphne, *querida*, this is my stepsister, Ana-Maria.'

Tawny eyes so wide open that the whites showed all around the golden irises stared at Daphne, who made an effort to smile again.

'*Buenas noches*, Ana-Maria,' she said, thinking she was beginning to sound like a parrot saying the same phrases over and over again.

'Your . . . your wife?' exclaimed Ana-Maria, swinging round to face Carlos, completely ignoring Daphne. '*No entiendo*—I don't understand. Why are you married to her?' She changed suddenly to Spanish words pouring out of her so fast that it sounded as if she was talking gibberish. Then, almost choking with fury, she raised her hand as if to hit Carlos across the face. But he was too quick for her, caught her wrist easily and bent her arm back. Wrenching her wrist free, she swung round glared at Daphne, then with a sob whirled about and raced up the stairs. A few seconds later a door slammed.

Immediately Teresa spoke sharply to Carlos in Spanish obviously rebuking him. He answered in the same language, his voice cold, and shrugged his shoulders. Teresa looked troubled and shook her head from side to side, then turned to Daphne.

'Please forgive Ana's display of temper,' she said. 'She's highly strung and she's always been very fond of Carlos. It was a shock to her to learn he's married. She's always hoped. . . .'

'That's enough, Madre,' Carlos cut in roughly. 'Daphne doesn't need to know all the details. We have come a long way today and are hungry. Do you have any supper for us?'

The dining room where they ate had the same faded French elegance of the hallway. Long green and silver brocade curtains hung at the two shuttered windows and a thin green and grey carpet covered the floor. The highly-polished oval table was set with lace mats, silver cutlery, delicate porcelain and glass. The dining chairs had carved arms and legs, oval padded backs and cushioned seats. Everything indicated that at one time the Fontaine family had been wealthy and had lived in luxury.

But the food which Teresa Fontaine served was uncompromisingly Mexican, the *chili* hot and spicy, thick with beans and chunks of beef. Carlos and his mother talked casually about ranch matters and Daphne spoke only when Teresa asked her a question about herself. She answered the questions truthfully as Carlos had told her to, and Teresa listened politely, making no comment at all.

Ana-Maria didn't appear again, and before Daphne and Carlos left the house to return to the bungalow Teresa apologised once again for the behaviour of her stepdaughter.

'But she will see you tomorrow,' she said, 'and will make friends with you.'

Although her mind was teeming with questions about Ana-Maria Daphne held her tongue on the walk back to the bungalow, keeping her resolve not to get involved. The stars were bigger, glowing in a black sky like yellow lamps. Grasshoppers sang in the undergrowth and there was a strong scent of sage on the wind which whistled a reedy tune in the grass. Somewhere far off, a bull bellowed and from the long bunkhouse came the sound of a guitar being plucked.

After the elegance of the French ranch house the bungalow seemed very bare and utilitarian, in great need of a woman's touch, thought Daphne, glancing round the living room. But it wasn't her concern. She was there to be Carlos's wife in front of other people only.

'I'm going over to see José,' Carlos announced coolly. 'Goodnight.'

'Goodnight,' she replied, equally cool, and drifted, with a sense of relief because for a while she would be alone, towards the bedroom. Would he join her in the wide low bed later? she wondered as, after undressing and slipping into her nightgown, she climbed into it. She would be asleep when he came, she would make sure of that.

There was a hollow in the middle of the bed, made she assumed by his body, and she rolled into it. Determinedly she dragged herself out of it, holding on to the edge of the mattress to prevent herself from slipping back into the dip. The sheets were clean but rough, made from coarse cotton which scratched her skin and the pillow was hard as if filled with straw. Such contrasts she thought sleepily, remembering the beautiful lace and brocade she had seen in the ranch house.

A vision of Ana-Maria swam before her mind's eye. The girl had been wearing a black dress which could only have been created in Paris. Beautiful, elegant, the wealthy heiress to the Fontaine ranch—why had she been so angry when Carlos had told her he was married?

Stop it, Daphne warned herself. *Stop wondering and imagining. You're here to do a job, not to ask questions. Don't get involved. Turn your mind off these people. In a month you'll be gone from here, you'll be going back to Wales where you'll forget them.*

CHAPTER FOUR

'DAPHNE, I'm going now.'

The voice wasn't the one she had been expecting to hear. It wasn't Elsa's, honeyed with pretended sweetness. It was masculine, softly gruff yet with an underlying toughness warning the listener that the speaker meant what he said and would brook no argument.

Coming up out of the shadows of the dream she had been having, Daphne opened her eyes. Carlos was sitting on the side of the bed, a dark shape silhouetted against the pale apricot light of sunrise which was slanting in through the window behind him. Wearing the white shirt and grey pants he had worn the night before, he held a white sombrero in one hand. His other hand was just sliding away from her bare shoulder which he had shaken to waken her.

'Going?' she repeated sleepily, and sat up. 'Going where?'

The bed sheet fell away from her shoulders. One strap of her nightgown had slipped down over one arm, exposing the swell of her breast. Carlos's dark glance swerved from her face downwards, and selfconsciously she pulled the strap up and over her shoulder.

'I'm going to look at the cattle,' he told her 'I'll be away all today and tonight as well.'

He was going away, leaving her on her own to cope with those two women at the ranch house. For three days and nights he had been with her, telling her what to do and say, protecting her, and now he was going away. Still drowsily vulnerable in the early morning, she didn't want to be parted from him yet and wasn't ready to face the day without him.

'Couldn't I come with you?' she asked surprising herself by the request.

'Can you ride a horse?' He was surprised by her question, too, she could tell by the way his eyebrows lifted.

'No, I can't.'

'Then you can't come with me, because that's how I'm travelling, on horseback,' he replied.

'Where will you stay tonight?'

'We'll camp out.'

'Who's we?'

'José and I and some of the ranch hands.'

'What shall I do all day, here by myself?' she asked, feeling panic flicker through her at the thought of having to deal with Teresa and Ana-Maria.

'Whatever you like. Do whatever it is that wives do all day,' he taunted.

He began to get to his feet, and impulsively, driven by some deep uncontrollable instinct, Daphne put a hand on his arm. Her fingers spread out over the coarse cotton of his shirt sleeve and she felt his muscle tense. He sat down again, his glance on her hand, his eyes hidden by thick jet-black lashes.

'*Que pasa?*' he demanded sharply. She had learned that he always spoke in his mother tongue when he was disturbed. He looked up, his eyes narrowing warily as they met her wide appealing glance.

'I . . . I'll miss you, Carlos,' she whispered. It wasn't what she had intended to say, but she could find no other way to express her sudden fear of being left alone in that alien place or to show him that she had valued his strength and protection during the past few days. His eyes widened, and one black eyebrow flickered upwards satirically.

'I thought you'd be glad to have a bed to yourself for a night,' he drawled.

'Please don't make fun. I . . . I mean it. I'll miss you.'

Lashes covered his eyes again as his glance drifted down from her eyes to her mouth. To Daphne it seemed that the space separating them throbbed suddenly with unspoken primitive needs. Her heart swelled in her breast and a sensation of dizziness washed over her. But it couldn't be the effect of high altitude here because the ranch was only about two hundred feet above sea level. She swayed towards him, her lips parting invitingly, lifting towards his. She saw his lips part too, their hard straight line softening as they quivered sensually. Then his breath came out in a hot gusty sigh to fill her mouth as his lips crushed hers in a violent kiss which gave her no chance to respond.

Back against the pillow she sank, pushed there by his weight although she went willingly, her hands lifting to his neck, her fingers playing in the thick tawny hair at his nape. Her lips bruised and squashed by the pressure of his, she felt she might be smothered at any minute. There was a sharp tingling sensation in one of her breasts and she realised that his fingers were there, stroking and pinching. Her mind reeled, her body arched uncontrollably against his. Time became of no account as a desperate burning desire seemed to fuse them together.

Her nightgown was tearing with a hissing sound when the thumping noise on the front door interrupted them. The knocking was followed by a man's voice shouting in Spanish. Carlos lifted his head. For a moment he stared down at her, little fires smouldering in the blackness of his eyes, his hands still curving about her breasts, and she couldn't be sure whether the thumping noise she could hear was her heart beating excitedly or someone knocking on the front door.

Suddenly Carlos rolled away from her, his booted feet thudding on the stone floor as he stood up.

'Was that what you wanted?' he asked harshly, not turning to look at her as he stuffed his shirt into the waistband of his pants and began to buckle his belt.

Gasping for breath, one forearm across her face to hide it, Daphne groaned.

'I . . . I . . . don't know,' she whispered. 'I don't know.'

'So if you don't know what it is you want don't try a trick like that again,' he rebuked her coldly.

As the sense of what he was saying penetrated her dazed mind Daphne sat up, pushing the thick hair back from her hot forehead. Carlos was striding towards the bedroom door, the white sombrero pulled down on his head, a navy blue short denim jacket slung over one shoulder. He went through the door, his booted feet beating a retreat along the passageway. Flinging herself out of bed, one hand clutching the shreds of her nightgown together across her breasts, Daphne ran barefooted after him.

'Wait—oh, please wait!' she cried, running into the living room.

About to open the front door, he turned and looked back at her. In the shadow of the hat brim his eyes were as enigmatic as ever, pools of unfathomable darkness.

'What now?' he drawled with a touch of impatience.

'I . . . I have to tell you,' she whispered, stopping by one of the bamboo chairs, gripping the back of it with her free hand. 'It . . . it wasn't a trick.'

His eyes narrowed to slits, his mouth hardened and he raised a hand to wipe the back of it across his lips as if to wipe away the feeling her lips had left on them. Then, shrugging his shoulders, he turned away to open the door.

'*Hasta la vista, amiga,*' he drawled indifferently, and stepping out on the verandah slammed the door after him. For a moment Daphne stood rigid, wondering at the pain which was slicing through her in reaction to his cool rejection of her explanation, then she moved forward to stand beside the window, hidden from the view of anyone outside but able to see Carlos mounting a beautiful dark red horse. Lariats and a water bottle hung from the saddle, which was leather decorated with silver studs. Nearby José, seeming wider and swarthier than ever in the morning light, sat on another horse, lighter in colour. José's short jacket was decorated also with silver studs and he wore a bright coloured scarf around his neck. As soon as Carlos was settled in the saddle José kneed his horse into movement, the reins held high in one hand, his other hand on his hip. Carlos followed him, sitting casually, long legs straight, his broad shoulders swaying slightly to the rhythm of the horse's walk, and together the two men passed out of sight beyond the dark shape of a barn.

Sighing, Daphne turned and hurried down the passageway to the bedroom. She picked up her watch from the chest of drawers. Half past six— too early for her to get up. She would lie down for another half hour. But as she approached the bed, saw the tumbled sheets and pillows, all that had happened there recently came rushing into her mind. She glanced down at her nightgown and groaned.

Oh, God, what on earth had come over her? Why had she behaved like a real wife, inviting her husband to kiss her before he left for work? Sinking down on the edge of the bed, she clutched her head between her hands, writhing inwardly in an agony of shame.

It was because she had been in need of comfort and reassurance, she argued with herself, that she had swayed against Carlos, offering her lips to him, and she had expected to receive a kiss like that other one he had given her when she had agreed to marry him in Taxco to prevent the police from putting him in jail. She had expected his kiss to be cool but friendly too, showing his appreciation of what she was doing to help him by pretending to be his wife. She hadn't expected the savage possession of her lips which she had just experienced.

Delicious tingles danced along her nerves creating a knot of excitement somewhere near the pit of her stomach, and groaning again, tormented by the physical sensations Carlos had aroused, she fell sideways across the bed. Gently she felt her breasts. They were taut with the desire to be touched again. In a few moments he had roused her as no other man had done. Mitchell Gardner's uninvited caresses had always sickened her. As for the kisses of Ellis, the young man she had gone about with in Swansea, they had been of the schoolboy variety, exploratory, but shy and inexperienced, like her own.

But Carlos had kissed her this morning with all the passion of a strong, healthy man who had wanted a woman and she guessed that if José had not thumped on the door and had called to him he would have taken her, whether she had been willing or not. And she had been willing, she had no doubts about that—very willing. She had wanted him—or at least she had wanted to find out with him the mystery of the consummation of marriage. She had wanted him to treat her as a man would treat his real wife.

Heat flooded through her body and she groaned again. Carlos had believed her behaviour had been a trick and he had treated her as he would have treated any woman who had offered herself to him, without love or tenderness. Yet she had to admit she had liked the way he had kissed her and she had responded . . . or at least her body had.

But making love wasn't part of their arrangement. There was to be no physical or emotional involvement in their brief marriage, for the simple reason that it would be over soon. Daphne moaned again as she realised how close they had come in a few minutes to the culmination of passion and how the consequences of such an act would have affected her. Several weeks from now, back in Wales, she might have found herself to be pregnant, carrying the child of a stranger who lived here in Mexico, and all because both of them had given in to physical desire.

She mustn't let it happen again, she vowed. She must avoid being alone with Carlos in bedrooms and on beds. Today she would find a way up to the loft he had talked about, and if he wouldn't sleep there she would. Only when his mother or other relatives were about would she show him that she liked him and enjoyed being with him. Ah, what was she thinking?

Did she like him? Did she enjoy being with him? Was it possible to fall in love in the short time of three days with a foreigner, a man whose background and upbringing were so different from her own and who probably regarded women as objects to be used and manipulated for his own self-gratification?

No, she mustn't fall in love with Carlos. She mustn't even think about it. Sliding off the bed, she stripped off the torn nightgown and dressed quickly in a wrap-around cotton skirt and a V-necked cotton top. Most of her clothes needed washing and she suspected the same was true of Carlos's too. How did one wash clothes in this bungalow? Was there such a thing as a washing machine? And how did one cook? It was time she found out.

Her arms full of soiled underwear, blouses, shirts and cotton slacks, she went down the passage to the living room, surprising a small dark young woman who had just entered the bungalow carrying a bucket and a mop.

'*Buenos dias,*' said Daphne, smiling, guessing she was the Indian woman Carlos had told her about who came to clean the house every day.

Her black eyes rounded in fear, the young woman dropped the bucket and the mop to the floor and muttering to herself in some strange language crossed herself several times before turning on her heel and running from the house, leaving the door wide open.

Tossing the pile of clothes on to the nearest chair, Daphne hurried after the woman, down the steps of the verandah.

'Come back!' she called, but the woman kept on running, her bare brown feet flashing below the hem of her full cotton skirt, her thick pigtail of black hair bouncing up and down on her back as she covered the hard-baked dusty ground and disappeared round the end of the barn. Daphne followed, coming to a stop when she reached the corral in front of the barn. Several boys, all of them wearing faded blue jeans and white T-shirts and sombrero hats, were perched on the top rail of the corral. Several pairs of dark eyes stared at Daphne in astonishment and then all the boys were sliding down off the rail and running after the woman shouting at the tops of their voices.

By the time Daphne reached the steps going up to the verandah in front of the old ranch house Teresa Fontaine was stepping out of the front door to see what the commotion was about.

'*Que pasa?*' she demanded sharply, her eyebrows slanting fiercely, reminding Daphne that this strong-looking, golden-skinned, dark-eyed woman was Carlos's mother.

'She ran away,' Daphne said breathlessly, and pointed towards the young woman with the pigtail who had stopped running and was surrounded by the boys. 'She took one look at me and ran away.'

'Who? Bonita? The girl who cleans house for Carlos?' queried Teresa, shading her eyes with one hand to look in the direction Daphne was pointing. 'Didn't Carlos tell you about her?'

'He told me about her, but I think he didn't tell her about me,' said Daphne dryly.

Teresa began to laugh. It started as a deep rumble in her ample chest and grew into an infectious chuckle which made her black eyes sparkle and her remarkably good teeth shine.

'Then I'm not surprised she ran away,' she gasped. 'She would be frightened when she saw you, with your yellow hair and your blue eyes. She would think you were a bad spirit from another world come to torment her. The Totonacs—and she is one—are very superstitious.'

Turning away from Daphne, Teresa cupped her hands about her mouth and shouted something. The girl and the boys looked up. Teresa waved an arm indicating that they were to come to her and slowly they began to walk back, dust scuffing up from beneath their feet. When they reached the bottom of the verandah steps they stopped and stared up at Daphne.

Teresa spoke to them in the strange language Daphne had heard the girl speaking, one hand gesturing towards Daphne, obviously explaining to them who she was. Then shyly, in obedience to her orders, they all trooped up the wide wooden steps of the verandah and shook hands with Daphne one by one and wished her good morning and welcome. Teresa spoke to them sharply again and they scattered like leaves before wind, scampering down the steps and disappearing behind the barn. Daphne would have followed, but Teresa spoke to her quickly.

'No, stay here. Let Bonita go and do the work. You stay here. Ana-Maria will be back soon. She went riding early.'

'I wanted to wash the clothes, Carlos's and mine—the ones we used on the journey here,' Daphne began vaguely. If she stayed there would be questions.

'Bonita will wash them. She does everything for Carlos.' Teresa smiled. 'I used to do the same for his father, Juan, when he came here to be manager.' Her smile became wistful as she reminisced. 'I was barely eighteen. He seemed like a god to me, with his fair hair and his grey eyes. He was a free spirit, strong yet gentle too. He knew so much about the land and about animals. There was no one like him, no one, and I loved him very much.' Teresa's dark eyes filled with tears and Daphne felt her eyes prick too in sympathy. 'When he died I thought I would die too. But I didn't.' Her mouth trembled as she tried to smile again. 'Have you had breakfast yet?' she asked.

'No, I haven't.'

'Then come in and have some in the kitchen and we will get to know each other.'

'I should go back to the bungalow,' Daphne murmured. 'There are things I should do. . . .'

'No, no, leave Bonita to do it all. You are not acclimatised yet,' said Teresa. 'It would not be good for you to work too hard at first in the heat.' She took hold of Daphne's arm and guided her towards the door. 'I am glad Carlos is married at last. For a long time I pray to the Virgin for his marriage because it isn't good for a man to stay single as long as he has. It's time he had a son and a daughter and it's long past time that I became a grandmother. You would like to have a baby, Daphne?'

'I . . . er . . . yes, I would,' Daphne muttered, feeling a twinge of conscience. Teresa seemed so sincerely pleased by Carlos's marriage to herself that she was beginning to feel guilty about the masquerade.

The kitchen was a big room equipped, much to Daphne's surprise, with modern electrical appliances and gadgets. At one end near a window was a round table set with a checked tablecloth on which there was already a place set for someone. After telling Daphne to sit at the table Teresa began to heap coffee grounds into a coffee-maker and soon the room was filled with the tantalising smell.

'Here is the fruit juice,' said Teresa, coming across to the table with a big glass jug of orange juice. 'Help yourself to cereal and milk. You like for me to cook you some eggs?'

'No, thank you. Cereal is fine, thank you,' said Daphne stiffly. It was a long time since anyone had mothered her.

'The coffee won't be long,' said Teresa, and sat down in the chair on the opposite side of the table to watch Daphne pour some juice into a glass. 'At first I think you are *nortamericana*,' Teresa continued, 'but you speak different. Your voice is soft and it sings. Where you come from?'

'From Wales, in Great Britain.'

'So!' Teresa drawled the word out and her black eyes went wide. 'That is a long way from here. And are you a lady like the daughter-in-law of your Queen?'

'Oh, no,' said Daphne quickly, laughing a little. 'I'm a commoner.' She saw puzzlement in Teresa's face and explained, 'My people belong to the working class. My father was a coalminer. He dug in a mine for coal.'

'*Si*, I understand,' Teresa nodded. 'My people are workers, too. My father was a farmer and he fought in the Revolution to get his land.'

'But how do you know about the Queen's daughter-in-law?' asked Daphne.

'I read about her in the newspaper and I watch part of her wedding on the television news.'

'You have television here?' exclaimed Daphne.

'But of course. We have everything here,' said Teresa complacently. 'Claude Fontaine was once a wealthy man. He died a few months ago, but his will is not settled yet. We do not know who own the ranch until it is settled. He have no direct heirs, you see.'

'But I thought Ana-Maria. . . .' Daphne began, breaking off when she saw Teresa shake her head from side to side.

'Ana-Maria is his first wife's daughter, not his own daughter. She is his stepdaughter just as Carlos is his stepson. You understand?'

'I think so.'

'But Carlos did not explain this to you?' Teresa looked surprised.

'No. He told me only that Ana-Maria is getting a divorce.'

'That is so. And now the divorce is through, so she come here looking for sympathy.' Teresa looked irritated. 'She was hoping. . . .' She broke off, shrugging. 'But Carlos said I was not to bore you with details,' she added, and reaching out across the table she touched the thick wave of hair that fell across Daphne's forehead. 'Your hair is pretty, like gold. I think I guess why Carlos choose you to be his wife—he likes the way you look. Do you like the way he look?'

'Er . . . yes, I do,' muttered Daphne. 'He's handsome . . . in a different way.'

'He's a mixture, hmm? A little bit Mexican like me and a lot of *gringo* like Juan, on the outside. But inside I think he is mostly like my father, Luis Valdez. Like my father Carlos will fight for what he believes belongs to him, just as my father fought for freedom and land in the Revolution.

Carlos will do anything to get what he wants—anything. And that is why he has married at last.' Teresa's black eyes blazed with a fierce light.

'What do you mean?' asked Daphne, feeling that she was close to finding out why Carlos needed a temporary wife. 'What will he get that he wants now that he is married?'

'He will become the owner of the Fontaine ranch,' whispered Teresa triumphantly. 'And at last the land will belong to us.' She glanced round at the door and began to rise to her feet. 'But I think I hear Ana-Maria coming in from her ride. It would be in your interests to be friendly towards her and not offend her in any way—she makes a spiteful enemy. The coffee is ready now.'

Teresa was pouring coffee into cups when Ana-Maria walked into the room. Dressed in hip-hugging dark blue jeans, a white silk blouse and riding boots, she carried a small whip in one hand. Her thick chestnut hair was tied back from her face and a flat-crowned, wide-brimmed hat hung on her shoulders from a cord round her neck. She wished Teresa a cool good morning and turned towards the breakfast table, checking and stiffening when she saw Daphne. But her hesitation was brief. Her lips curving into a smile which showed her small white teeth, she pulled out a chair from the table and extended a long-fingered hand.

'My behaviour last night was *guache*,' she said. 'I hope you forgive it.'

'You were upset and surprised,' said Daphne, politely shaking the slim hand.

'I was more than that,' said Ana-Maria, her

finely plucked eyebrows arching. 'I was angry. You see. . . .' She broke off, catching her lower lip between her teeth, her long lashes sweeping down to cover her eyes. 'No importa,' she murmured. 'Carlos is and always has been very dear to me. Ever since I remember he is here on the ranch. He teach me to ride. He teach me to speak English. He teach me many things. He and I have been close—like that.' She held up two fingers of her right hand and crossed one over the other, and her glance challenged Daphne. 'We have been closer than any real brother and sister in the past—and yet he did not tell me about you when I was here a few months ago for my stepfather's funeral. He never mention you at all. Where did you and he meet?'

'In Acapulco.'

'When?'

'Last year.'

'Carlos went there for a holiday last year and again this year,' put in Teresa. 'You know, Ana-Maria, how he likes to have a complete change from ranch life, the bright lights, the dancing and music and. . . .'

'The beautiful women,' suggested Ana-Maria dryly, her voice drawling slightly. 'Yes, I know. But what were you doing in Acapulco, Daphne? Were you on holiday there too?'

'No. I was working there. I . . . I'm a hairdresser and I've been working as a personal maid to a film star for over a year now. She has a house in Acapulco. You may have heard of her . . . Elsa Thomas.' Daphne hoped she sounded convincing.

She had decided to keep her relationship to Elsa to herself.

'*Si*, I have heard of her,' said Ana-Maria, picking up a coffee cup and nursing it between her hands while she studied Daphne over the rim, her golden eyes very hard and penetrating.

'A hairdresser?' exclaimed Teresa, clapping her hands together in delight. 'Do you have your tools with you? Your scissors and your blow-dryer?'

'Yes, I do have them with me.'

'Then you can dress my hair for me,' said Teresa enthusiastically. 'Wash it, cut it and arrange it. While Carlos was away I had no time to go into the town to visit *la sala de belleza*. How you say that in English?' she demanded, turning to Ana.

'The beauty salon,' replied Ana smoothly, putting down her cup, her gaze never wavering from Daphne's face. 'You will certainly be popular here, Daphne,' she continued. 'Mexican women do not like to do their own hair and there are more beauty shops per square mile in this country than any other country. Maybe you would fix my hair too.'

'I would like to,' said Daphne, remembering Teresa's recent advice that she shouldn't offend Ana-Maria.

'And in return I'll teach you to ride,' said Ana-Maria with a smile. 'This morning I ride with Carlos and José as far as the river and Carlos told me that you didn't go with him today because you can't ride, so I promised I would show you how while he is away and then the next time he goes range-riding you'll be able to ride with him. Would you like to do that?'

The offer seemed sincere. How should she answer? How would Carlos's real wife answer? Daphne knew how she wanted to answer. She wanted to learn to ride. As a child she had wanted to have riding lessons at the nearby riding school, but had not been able to afford them.

'Yes, I would like to learn,' she said. 'But I don't have the right clothes. I've no riding breeches or hat.'

'Ah, you are thinking of learning to ride in the English style,' said Ana-Maria. 'But we do not ride like that on the range. We ride Mexican style, which is now known as Western. It was the Mexican *charro* or cowboy who taught the American cowboys what they know about riding and gave them many of their terms ... rodeo, lasso, corral, lariat, stampede ... to name a few. The *charro* is a model of elegance and charm afoot but a demon in the saddle. And there are *charras* too, hard-working hard-riding girls who put on shows called *charreadas* regularly. You should go to see one. But meantime all you need to go riding is a tough pair of jeans and some boots.'

'I have jeans but no boots,' said Daphne.

'What size do you take?'

'An eight in American sizing.'

'No problem,' said Ana-Maria smiling again. 'You can borrow a pair of mine. I take the same size. So, we begin right now, if you have finished your breakfast?' she said, rising to her feet.

'I would like to,' said Daphne. 'But perhaps I should ...' her voice trailed away uncertainly because she had no idea what she would do if she didn't do as Ana-Maria suggested.

'Perhaps you are afraid of horses,' said Ana-Maria challengingly.

The challenge was all Daphne needed. She wasn't going to have this rather snobbish Franco-Mexican woman thinking she was afraid of anything.

'No, I'm not afraid. In fact I've always wanted to ride a horse.'

'Then go and get into your jeans and I'll go and get the boots. I'll bring them to the bungalow.' Swinging round, Ana-Maria strode purposefully towards the kitchen door.

'You will be careful, Ana-Maria,' Teresa called after her. 'I would not like Daphne to be hurt while Carlos is away. He would be very angry with me if I let anything happen to her.'

In the doorway Ana-Maria turned to look back across the room, her eyebrows arching scornfully.

'What could possibly happen to her?' she drawled. 'Today she will practise here in the corral where you can watch over her if you like. Carlos told me which horse she should learn to ride on. It's the mare called Black Velvet. She is gentle and patient. Okay?'

'I suppose so,' murmured Teresa, frowning, turning to the breakfast table and beginning to gather up the used plates.

'Then I get the boots and see you in ten

minutes, Daphne,' said Ana-Maria determinedly, and went from the room.

'You'll take care, Daphne,' said Teresa. 'I know I warned you not to offend Ana-Maria, but you can refuse to learn riding. You can say you would prefer to wait for Carlos to return and teach you.' Teresa's mouth quivered uncontrollably and her dark eyes filled with tears. 'I hate horses,' she muttered. 'Ever since the day my Juan was killed I have hated the brutes.'

'I understand,' Daphne said consolingly. 'But I would like to learn to ride while I'm here.'

'You are not staying?' Teresa was quick—too quick, thought Daphne ruefully as she realised she had made a slip.

'Oh, yes, yes, of course I'm staying. I meant I would like to learn to ride while Ana-Maria is here to teach me, because when he returns Carlos might be too busy with his work to give me lessons and I would like to go with him next time he goes riding the range. I think the wife of a rancher should be able to ride, don't you?'

To her relief Teresa nodded and smiled, although there was still an expression of anxiety in her eyes.

'I can see you love my son and want to be a good wife to him,' she said. 'I am glad he found you, Daphne, but I have to admit you are very different from what I expected.'

'Oh. What did you expect?'

'Someone older, harder, more experienced. You seem very young and innocent. I would not like to see you hurt by anyone, least of all by Carlos. I hope you can handle him. He is what we call one tough *hombre*. Go now and change into your jeans or Ana-Maria will be going to the bungalow with your boots and not finding you there.'

So far so good, thought Daphne, as she walked back to the bungalow. She must be a better actress than she had thought if she had already convinced Teresa that she loved Carlos and wanted only to be a good wife to him. And she had only slipped up once during the course of conversation with Teresa and Ana-Maria when she had said she would like to learn riding while she was staying here.

Carlos' shirts, her blouses and their underwear were fluttering in the hot dry wind from a line which was looped between one end of the bungalow to a post set in the ground a few yards away. Bonita had been busy already. Inside the house was neat and clean, smelling slightly of disinfectant. The bed was made and the shutters had been closed over the bedroom window to keep the sunrays out during the middle of the day.

With someone to do the housework staying on the ranch for the next few weeks pretending to be Carlos's wife was going to be more of a holiday than anything else, she thought as she pulled on her jeans. A holiday with pay, with riding lessons thrown in, she thought with a little laugh. All she had to do was say as little as possible and pretend she loved Carlos . . . in front of others only, of course.

Ana-Maria's boots were on the tight side since Daphne's foot was wider, but they went on, and since she wouldn't be walking much in them

Daphne decided she could manage in them. For the next two hours she practised mounting and dismounting and riding round the corral, learning how to make the horse go and how to make it stop by using the reins and her knees. Ana-Maria was a good teacher, giving instructions in a clear but firm way as she sat perched on the top rail of the corral, and Daphne, being keen to ride, learnt quickly, so that by lunch-time she was able to ride Black Velvet at a trot round the corral.

'Later this afternoon, when it is cooler, we shall go for a short ride together,' Ana-Maria said after ordering one of the ranch hands to lead the horse away and unsaddle it. 'And tomorrow maybe we ride farther, go to meet Carlos returning, give him a surprise. You would like that?'

'I would like that,' said Daphne with a little laugh. 'He will be so surprised.'

'He will be *very* surprised,' said Ana-Maria, also laughing as she hooked her arm through Daphne's in a friendly way. 'And now let's go in and have lunch.'

After lunch Teresa insisted that Daphne take a rest.

'We do not normally keep *siesta* on the ranch because people who work on the land have to use all the daylight there is. But you are not yet used to the heat.'

Much to her own surprise Daphne slept almost two hours that afternoon and wakened feeling thoroughly rested although a little stiff in the muscles she had used when riding. Remembering her promise to wash and cut Teresa's hair, she found her scissors, combs and her blow-dryer and walked over to the house. An hour later when Teresa's hair was smooth and shining and coiled into an attractive style, Daphne pulled on Ana-Maria's spare riding boots and went riding again, this time outside the corral. Mounted on a beautiful buckskin horse, Ana-Maria rode beside her along a track which curved across the land to a line of rustling acacia trees edging a wide shallow river, where the grass was long and lush and a group of cattle had gathered to shelter from the heat of the sun in the afternoon.

'Tomorrow we'll ride beside the river towards the mountains because I think Carlos will come back that way,' Ana-Maria said, as they reined in. She pointed to the hills with her whip. 'Up there is the site of an excavation. Archaeologists from the National Institute of Anthropology and History in Mexico City are uncovering the evidence of the very earliest human occupancy of this area. So far they have found remains and artifacts as old as 2900 B.C. Maybe we ride that far tomorrow and you will see the site. But now we go back and you do my hair.'

Ana-Maria turned her horse in a graceful circle and began to ride back in the direction of the ranch buildings. Holding her reins in the same way, Daphne tried to turn Black Velvet, but the mare stubbornly refused to move no matter how often Daphne pressed with her knees or talked to her. At last, realising Daphne was not with her, Ana-Maria turned and rode back and taking hold of the mare's reins pulled the horse round, leading it after her as she rode towards the ranch house again.

'She is a little stubborn this one, when she gets tired,' she said, and added laughingly, 'And like most women she likes to have her own way. I like to have my own way, don't you, Daphne?'

'Within reason,' replied Daphne noncommittally.

'Mmm. How cool you are, a typical Northerner with your reasonable attitude,' Ana-Maria jeered lightly. 'No Latin fire in you, no fierce determination to get what you want. Supposing some woman tried to take Carlos away from you, what would you do? Would you fight to keep him?'

'It would depend on what he wanted,' Daphne replied evasively, glad she was behind Ana-Maria so that the other woman couldn't see the uncertainty expressed on her face.

Ana-Maria reined in and turned her horse so she could look at Daphne. In the rosy light of the setting sun her heart-shaped face with its arching eyebrows wore a mocking expression.

'Meaning, I suppose, if he wanted the other woman more than he wanted you you would let him go to her. You'd give in. You wouldn't fight,' she said tauntingly. 'Ha, it's as I thought—you do not love him. Then why have you married him? How did you trap him? Are you going to have his child?'

'No, no, I'm not,' retorted Daphne. 'I married him because he asked me to marry him.'

'When? When did he ask you?' demanded Ana-Maria, urging her horse nearer so that she could see Daphne's face more clearly.

'When . . . when he came to Acapulco . . . two . . . two weeks ago,' Daphne stuttered, disconcerted by the question.

'And weren't you surprised that he asked you?' persisted Ana-Maria.

'Yes, I was,' admitted Daphne. The answer was truthful and Ana-Maria could make of it what she liked.

'He should have waited,' mused Ana-Maria, her eyes slitted as she looked beyond Daphne. 'He should have waited and married me. That was what Papa wished, what he and I planned together.' Her teeth snapped together viciously as she pulled on the reins to turn her horse. 'But the old fool made a mistake when he wrote his will. Either that or Carlos. . . .' Ana-Maria broke off, shaking her head from side to side. '*No importa*,' she said, turning and smiling at Daphne. 'Take no notice of what I say. Come now, let's go in and you can do my hair. You think I should have it cut, hmm? In one of those new styles, like yours?'

CHAPTER FIVE

ALONE, in the middle of the wide bed, Daphne lay in the hollow which had been made by Carlos's body and listened to the night sounds coming through the shutters, the chant of cicadas; the rustle of grasses. Although every muscle in her body ached after riding she couldn't sleep because she kept thinking about what Ana-Maria had said about Carlos.

He should have waited and married me. That was what Papa wished, what he and I planned together. But the old fool made a mistake when he wrote his will.

What was the mistake Claude Fontaine had made? Daphne turned restlessly, wishing she could stop her questing thoughts. Surely it was enough for her to know that Carlos had married so that he could become owner of the ranch. She didn't need to know any more, and Carlos hadn't wanted her to know that much. Why hadn't he wanted her to know? Perhaps he had thought she would have refused to marry him if she had known he had wanted a temporary wife only to further his ambition.

Think about something else. Think about going home to Wales with money in her pocket, enough possibly to start her own beauty salon. Forget about Ana-Maria, about Teresa and the complications caused by the will of a man she had never known; the thin frail-looking aristocratic-looking Claude Fontaine, whose portrait hung with the portraits of other Fontaines in the old ranch house.

Forget, too, about Carlos. Forget the dark-eyed, secretive, determined man who would do anything to get what he wanted; who had married herself, paying her to do what he asked so he could inherit this ranch. She could understand now why Ana-Maria had been so angry last night when she had discovered he had married someone else.

She slept at last and wakened early to the sound of the wake-up whistle which roused the ranch workers every morning at sunrise. At once Carlos leapt into her mind. Today he would return, and she would be glad to see him.

The arrival of Bonita to clean and wash any soiled clothing reminded Daphne that she had done nothing about tidying the loft, so with the help of a Spanish phrase book and sign language she managed to convey to Bonita that she wanted to go up into the loft if she could only find a ladder. Understanding at last, the girl went out of the house, returning a few minutes later with one of the ranch hands who was carrying an aluminium extension ladder.

Obligingly the man propped the ladder against the edge of the opening in the kitchen ceiling and went up the ladder to slide the cut-out panel which covered the hole. When he came down both

Daphne and Bonita went up to look at what would have to be moved before the bed could be made. They were both up there, pushing boxes about, when a voice called out from the kitchen.

'Daphne? Daphne? Where are you?' The voice was Ana-Maria's.

'In the loft,' Daphne answered, feeling her stomach muscles tense. Ana-Maria had come, she guessed, to suggest they go riding and she wasn't sure whether she should go. Perhaps it would be wiser to stay and wait for Carlos to come back instead of going to meet him. He might not be pleased if she behaved too much like a real wife.

Keeping her head bent so that she wouldn't bang it in the sloping roof, she went to the hole in the floor of the loft and looked down. Her face upside down, Ana-Maria looked up from the bottom of the ladder.

'What are you doing?' she exclaimed.

'Carlos asked me to tidy the loft,' Daphne replied.

'And do you always do what Carlos tells you?' scoffed Ana-Maria. 'Are you one of those submissive wives, always at the beck and call of your husband? Come down, so we can talk properly. It's giving me a crick in my neck looking up at you.'

Reluctantly Daphne descended the ladder, patting dust from her clothing when she reached the floor.

'Why don't you let Bonita tidy the loft for you?' asked Ana-Maria as they moved from the kitchen into the living room.

'I don't know how to ask her,' said Daphne with a touch of impatience. 'It's taken me half an hour to ask her to find me a ladder—I don't know enough Spanish.'

'Then I'll tell her for you, if you like. What is it you want doing?'

'I'd like everything arranging up there so that it's possible to use the bed. I'd also like clean sheets and a blanket putting on the bed.'

'Why?' demanded Ana-Maria. 'Are you expecting a house guest?'

'No. Carlos and I . . . well, we just thought it would be nice to have a spare bedroom,' replied Daphne stiffly, wiping sweat from her forehead on her arm. It had been hot and stuffy in the small loft. Sleeping up there would not be comfortable.

'So I will tell Bonita what it is you want and you can get ready for your riding lesson,' said Ana-Maria coolly. 'Where is she?'

'In the loft.'

The riding lesson lasted an hour and during that time Daphne learned to urge Black Velvet into a canter. When she had cantered round the corral several times to Ana-Maria's satisfaction, Ana-Maria suggested that they go into the house for a cool drink and something to eat.

'You're really making progress,' she said encouragingly. 'Carlos should be coming back now. Shall we go and meet him?'

'Now?' exclaimed Daphne. 'But isn't it too hot to go riding?'

'Not really. We can keep close to the river and

ride in the shade of the trees. We can reach the excavation site I told you about in half an hour. Come on, come with me. I'll think you're chicken if you don't, and I shall tell Carlos that you are.'

'All right,' said Daphne. For some reason she didn't want Ana-Maria riding to meet Carlos alone. A strange distrust of the other girl was building up inside her, based on a certain amount of jealousy because Ana-Maria talked about Carlos so intimately and had hoped to marry him. 'But I shall have to have a hat.'

'I have a sombrero you can borrow,' replied Ana-Maria easily. 'And now let's find out what Teresa has prepared for lunch.'

There were *tacos* filled with highly spiced meat to eat. Daphne would have preferred something less spicy, but there didn't seem to be anything else, and the fieriness in her mouth left by the spices was washed away by the light lager type beer Teresa provided. Half an hour later, astride Black Velvet, she was following Ana-Maria on the buckskin across the wide field towards the river.

It was pleasant riding under the shade of the rustling acacia trees beside the sliding silvery waters of the river. The tinkle of water against rocks, the juicy greenness of the long grasses, created an impression of coolness. But it did not last for long because, swerving aside from the course of the river, Ana-Maria urged her horse along a path that climbed steadily through a rough terrain of rocks and cacti towards a plateau a few hundred feet above the river where, she told Daphne, the archaeological camp was situated.

The sun beat down mercilessly. Perspiration ran down Daphne's cheeks and soaked her blouse. Her stomach was beginning to feel a little queasy, the after-effects of the *taco* she had eaten for lunch, she was sure, having learned the hard way that the hot, spicy Mexican foods sometimes disagreed with her. She was also beginning to feel a little saddle-sore.

Yet Ana-Maria, still riding slightly ahead, looked cool and fresh as if she had just set out. With her attractive flat-crowned hat tilted forward slightly to shade her eyes, her back straight, her body moving with casual grace as her horse picked its way between the rocks, she looked as if she could go on riding all day.

The path they had been following widened into a small glade formed by huge boulders of rocks and some straggling trees.

'Would you mind if we stopped here for a while?' Daphne asked huskily. Her throat felt parched. 'I'd like to have a drink of water.'

'Of course.' Ana-Maria reined in willingly, turning her horse. She slid from the saddle and pulled the reins over the head of the buckskin so that they trailed on the ground and the animal wouldn't wander away. Then she began to take a water bottle from the leather slot that attached it to her saddle. Daphne dismounted awkwardly, feeling every joint creak, and also pulled the reins over the head of the black mare.

'Here you are,' said Ana-Maria, offering the water bottle. 'I wouldn't like you to die of thirst, and you so newly married.' There was a stinging quality to her voice, and Daphne glanced at her warily as she raised the water bottle to her lips. The water was tepid but eased her throat. Placing the stopper back on the bottle, she handed it back to Ana-Maria and sliding the sombrero back to her shoulders she tried to wipe the sweat from her forehead with her hands. With a hand resting on the saddle Ana-Maria stood by her horse, watching, her lips twisting in a slightly scornful smile.

'You're certainly not suited to live here in the Gulf region,' she drawled. 'It becomes disagreeably hot in the summer months and the rain can be torrential. This is only April.' Her golden eyes were hard as their glance raked Daphne's wilting figure. 'When summer comes, you'll go. You'll leave Carlos and will ask him for a divorce.'

Tempted to blurt out that she wouldn't be staying until the summer, Daphne checked herself just in time, realising that Ana-Maria was trying to goad her into making such a mistake. Straightening up, she tilted her chin, giving Ana-Maria look for look.

'Is that what you did?' she asked tauntingly. 'Did you sue your husband for divorce because you didn't like the climate where he lived?'

Ana-Maria's laugh was a shrill trill of mockery which grated on the nerves.

'No. I divorced Miguel for two reasons. Firstly because I was tired of him. He is rich but dull. Rich men often are boring as lovers, you know, because they are interested only in making money. My mother found that out about Claude too—

that was why she left him. He made a good settlement on her, but I managed to get more out of Miguel than she did out of Claude. I got two million—dollars, I mean, not *pesos*.' Ana-Maria looked very self-satisfied. 'The other reason I divorced him was because I wanted to marry Carlos.' Ana-Maria's tawny eyes grew sultry and her full lips pouted sensually. 'I have always fancied him as a lover,' she said, her husky voice purring.

'Then why didn't you marry him in the first place instead of Miguel?' asked Daphne. Ana-Maria was like some of Elsa's women friends; she had used marriage as a way of making money. But then, she thought miserably, wasn't that exactly what she was going to do? Hadn't she agreed to accept money from Carlos in return for being his wife for a short time?

'I didn't marry Carlos seven years ago because he wasn't around,' retorted Ana-Maria. 'Also he had nothing to offer then and Claude hadn't made him his heir. It was only after I had married Miguel that ... that *péon*, Teresa, began to put ideas into Claude's head, hinting that her son was the only person who could rescue the ranch from the mess it was in because he knew about cattle and the land; because this ranch was his natural heritage; because he is the only grandson of Luis Valdez. *Pa!*' Ana-Maria spat suddenly and viciously. 'Every day she said it, until Claude believed her and wrote in his will that Carlos was to inherit the ranch and half the Fontaine fortune on his death.'

'Who was to inherit the other half of his fortune?'

'It was to be split between Teresa and me,' said Ana-Maria bitterly. 'I was furious when Claude told me, and it was then I asked him to include a condition in his will.'

'What sort of condition?' asked Daphne. She felt very bewildered and her head was beginning to ache.

'I told Claude that he was being unfair to me because I had as much right to inherit the property and half the fortune as Carlos had. I pointed out to him that I had been much more a daughter to him than Carlos had been a son, for the simple reason that I had been his stepchild for longer than Carlos had. As I had hoped, he was very upset by my accusation and he agreed to put in his will that Carlos would only inherit the ranch and half the fortune if he married me before the end of six months after Claude's death. That gave me time to divorce Miguel, you see, if I happened to be still married to him when Claude died. It would have worked out perfectly, only the silly old fool forgot to include my name when he asked for the condition to be inserted in his will.' Ana-Maria made a grating sound in her throat and raising her clenched fists shook them. 'Oh, I could scream when I think of it!' she hissed.

'I'm not sure I understand,' said Daphne, one hand to her head. Everything seemed to be wavering before her eyes and she wondered whether it was the effect of the heat.

'When Claude died five and a half months ago

his lawyer produced his will. The condition had been written in and it stated clearly enough that Carlos could only inherit the ranch if he married before the end of six months had passed after Claude's death. But it didn't state the name of the woman he was to marry. My name wasn't included.' Ana-Maria ground her teeth together and glared viciously at Daphne. 'It implied that Carlos could marry any woman and inherit the ranch. It implied he could pick up any little chick in a place like Acapulco and marry her to get what he wanted and has always wanted, ownership of the Fontaine ranch. So he married you.'

Daphne could only stare for a few minutes, wondering if she had heard correctly. Then suddenly she saw the ridiculous side of the situation; she saw how a frail and forgetful old man had defeated Ana-Maria's ambition, and she began to laugh.

'Oh, how funny!' she spluttered. 'How very funny!'

'Funny?' exclaimed Ana-Maria, whirling round to face her. She raised her right hand which was holding her whip as if to strike Daphne, thought better of it and lowered it swiftly to her side, but her big eyes blazed with yellow fire. 'I didn't find it funny at the time, nor do I find it funny now. I told the lawyer that a mistake had been made and asked why my name had not been included, and he told me that Claude had never mentioned it when giving instructions for the condition to be inserted. I told Carlos also that Claude had wanted us to marry each other so that we would both inherit the ranch and the fortune and that I would be free to marry him within the six months.'

'What did he say to that?' asked Daphne.

'He told me to go ahead and get a divorce, and I assumed that when it was through he would marry me.' Ana-Maria's teeth glittered as her lips drew back in a snarl. 'He tricked me, and for that I'm going to make him pay!'

'Oh, no,' said Daphne urgently, made anxious by the expression on Ana-Maria's face. The girl looked as if she was out of her mind. 'It wasn't his fault that Claude forgot to put in your name.'

'Carlos didn't have to marry you,' said Ana-Maria through her teeth. 'He could have married me—that's what I can't forgive.'

'I . . . I'm sorry,' said Daphne placatingly. 'I didn't know or I wouldn't have. . . .' She broke off, realising that what she had been about to say was untrue. Even if she had known about Claude's will she would have married Carlos. She had married him to prevent the police from putting him in jail. 'Please, Ana-Maria, can't you forgive and forget?' she went on. 'I'm sure Carlos didn't marry me just to spite you.'

'But I know he did,' retorted Ana-Maria, heaving herself up into her saddle. 'Are you rested enough now to go on?'

'I'd really prefer to go back to the ranch house,' said Daphne. 'Or to rest here until it goes cooler and then return. I don't feel very well.'

Ana-Maria's lips curved scornfully and her eyes

slitted unpleasantly as she looked down her finely
chiselled nose.

'You really are soft, aren't you?' she taunted.
'All right, stay here and wait until it goes cooler.
I'm going on.'

She kicked her heels against her horse's belly
and the buckskin started forward, its hooves
scrabbling on loose stones as it took the incline
and disappeared behind one of the big boulders.
For a few moments Daphne stood looking in the
direction Ana-Maria had gone. Perhaps she
should follow. No, her head ached too much and
she felt very sickly. She would sit down in the
shade and wait for Ana-Maria's return.

Going to the black mare, she took the heavy
saddle off its back and the saddle blanket, then
led the horse to stand in the shade of one of the
big rocks. She heaved the saddle and blanket over
to the few trees, spread the blanket on the ground
and using the saddle as a pillow lay down. She
closed her eyes, but opened them again quickly
because when she closed them her head whirled.
Sitting up, she leaned her back against one of the
tree-trunks. She guessed what was wrong with
her. She had a touch of gastro-enteritis; it wasn't
the first time she had suffered from it since she
had been in Mexico. Once more she closed her
eyes. This time her head didn't whirl and slowly
her head dropped and she dozed.

It was a burning sensation on her face and on
her hands that wakened her with a start, and she
opened her eyes to find she was no longer sitting
in the shade and the sun was shining directly into

her eyes. Woozily she got to her feet and staggered over to the horse, which was also standing in full sunshine. Untying it, she led it to another patch of shade, then looked at her watch. It was almost five o'clock. No, it couldn't be. She peered closely at the watch, sure that she had made a mistake, but the fingers stayed where they had been. Ana-Maria had been gone nearly two hours.

Daphne turned to the horse, looking for the saddle and a water bottle. She had to have something to drink and then she would mount the horse and go and look for Ana-Maria. She remembered she had put the saddle under the trees and she wandered over to them, still staggering a little. She bent lifted the saddle up. There was no water bottle attached to it; there had never been any water bottle attached to it. Ana-Maria had the only water they had brought with them.

To get water she would have to return to the river. With the saddle in her arms she went back to the horse and managed to put the saddle on the animal's back. Bending to fasten the cinch under the mare's belly made her feel very ill, and it was a while before she had recovered sufficiently to take the reins in her hand and attempt to mount.

Somehow she managed to struggle up into the saddle. She lifted the reins, clicked her tongue and pressed the horse with her knees. Black Velvet didn't move. Its ears didn't even flick. Head drooping, shoulders slack, the animal just stood there.

'Oh, come on,' whispered Daphne desperately. 'Move!' She leaned forward, caressing the beast's neck with one hand and murmured into its ear,

'Please, Blackie, don't be stubborn. Take me back to the ranch house.'

The horse made no sign of having heard or understood, and Daphne realised ruefully that it probably only understood Spanish, so she kicked it with her heels as she had seen Ana-Maria kick her horse. The mare didn't flinch, nor did it rush forward as the buckskin had done.

'All right, I'll walk,' said Daphne defiantly. 'But you're going to come with me.' The words were hardly out of her mouth when the animal suddenly lurched forward, arched its back and kicked up its heels. Over its hunched head and shoulders Daphne sailed, somersaulting involuntarily to land on her back. All breath knocked out of her, her head reeling from the blow it had received when the back of it hit a hard rock, she lay there watching the sky whirl around above her.

After a while she managed to crawl over and lift herself to her hands and knees, then with a great effort she stood up. Everything, rocks, trees, ground and sky, seesawed about her. Slowly things settled down and she looked around for the black horse. It wasn't anywhere to be seen.

Walking as fast as she could in the tight high-heeled Western boots, Daphne went down the path, fully expecting to see Black Velvet when she turned the first bend. But the horse had a good start on her and it wasn't until she reached the bottom of the slope that she saw it cantering away across the grass towards the river.

Well, she couldn't blame it for wanting a drink,

because that was what she wanted too. Gritting her teeth against the sickness which was swelling up in her stomach and the hammer pain behind her eyes and at the back of her head, she set off across the field, aware of the sun blazing down on her neck and knowing that she had forgotten to pick up the sombrero after it had fallen from her head when the horse had thrown her.

But she wasn't aware she had fainted until she came round and found herself looking up at a pale green, crimson-flushed sky which was faintly pin-pricked with stars. To move and stand up and walk forward was agony, but she managed it, only to find she was completely disorientated and had no idea in which direction she should walk.

Make for the river, for the line of trees smudging the horizon—that was the way to go. Stumbling and swaying, she set off, only to fall down again. She felt very hot—hot and dry. If only she could get to the river! There she would be able to cool off, wade in the silvery water, drink it. Once again she scrambled to her feet and tried to walk on, and once again she fell down. This time she didn't bother to get up. It was much better to lie where she was even though she was being eaten alive by ants.

The sun went down. An evening breeze stirred the grasses. The heat faded from the air, but Daphne didn't move. Delirious with fever, she muttered occasionally, unintelligibly. She didn't hear the approach of a truck, nor did she hear it stop. She didn't hear or see the two men who got down from the truck to look at her. Not until one of them was carrying her towards the truck did she come round, then she opened her eyes and looked up and by the loom of light from the truck's headlamps saw blue eyes looking down at her out of a bearded face.

'Who are you?' she croaked, and the blue eyes widened with surprise.

'Tom Hutton. Who are you?'

'Daphne Thomas. I mean Daphne— Daphne. . . .' What on earth was her new surname? 'I'm married to Carlos,' she added weakly.

'Carlos Thomas?' asked the bearded man, and was interrupted by someone she couldn't see who said something she could hear. 'Do you live at the ranch house?' asked the bearded man, heaving her higher in his arms, preparing to lift her into the front seat of the truck.

'I live in a bungalow near the ranch house.'

'Then we'll take you there.'

She felt very sick when the truck began to move forward and she kept swaying about until the man with the board put an arm around her and held her close to his side.

'You're in a pretty bad way,' he said. 'What happened?'

'Are you from England?' she muttered. 'You sound English.'

'No, I'm a Canadian, from Toronto. But my mother is from England, so I guess I've picked up some English accent from her,' he replied easily.

'I'm Welsh,' she mumbled.

'So what are you doing lying on the ground in the middle of a Mexican ranch?'

'I'm married to Carlos.'

'Hmm, so you said. I guess he doesn't look after you too well.'

'My horse ran away. I was trying to go after it when I fell down.' It was a great effort to talk. The words kept running into each other.

'Good thing we came along when we did. We were on our way back to the site. We're arch-aeologists.'

'That's where Ana-Maria was going,' muttered Daphne.

'Who? The horse?'

'No—Ana-Maria. She said she would come back, but she didn't.'

'Okay, guess you'd better save your explana-tions for Carlos when we find him. Hey, slow down, Diego. I think I can see someone coming this way on a horse. Maybe whoever it is is look-ing for the lady.'

Hazily Daphne was aware of the truck slowing down and stopping. The man who wasn't holding her shouted a question to someone she couldn't see. Vaguely she heard a voice answer—she couldn't be sure, but it sounded like Carlos's voice. The truck trundled forward again, her head swayed and she lost consciousness.

She came round again when someone was carrying her, up some stairs. She opened her eyes and looked up. Light blazed from a pretty glass chandelier. Her gaze swerved away from the dazzling light to the face of the man carrying

carrying her. Black eyes under slanting brows
looked down at her warily.

'Carlos,' she whispered, and raised a weak hand
to touch his bristly chin. 'Oh, Carlos, I'm so glad
to see you! Ana-Maria and I rode out to meet you
. . . but my horse ran away. Did Ana-Maria meet
you?'

'No.'

'Then where is she? Is she here?'

'No.'

'Oh, you never say anything!' she moaned dis-
gustedly.

'And you talk too much,' he retorted, reaching
the top of the stairs and turning along a landing.

'Where are you taking me?' she asked.

'To bed.'

'In the loft?'

The black glance flashed down to her face, and
for a moment the straight line of his mouth
softened.

'No. In the ranch house. You are ill, *querida*,
and we must put you to bed and call a doctor.'

'What does *querida* mean?' she whispered,
turning her face against his chest, feeling the
warmth beating out from his body to her cheek.
Carlos didn't answer but laid her down on a bed
and stepped back. The last person she saw before
she lost consciousness again was Teresa, bending
over her, her lined brown face creased with concern, her black eyes anxious.

CHAPTER SIX

RAIN pinged incessantly on the corrugated iron roof of the bungalow, a perpetual drumming noise which would eventually numb the brain, thought Daphne, looking up from the book she was reading and grimacing at the window. All she could see through the glass was a wall of grey water. It had rained all day, blotting out views, turning pathways and yards into mud-baths, driving everyone indoors.

The book dropped from her lax hands on to her knee. It was the last day of April. She had been at the Fontaine ranch for two weeks and for seven days out of the fourteen she had been confined to bed in the ranch house with a severe attack of gastro-enteritis which had been complicated by sunstroke. For part of that time she had been feverish, slipping in and out of consciousness, only vaguely aware of Teresa hovering over her like a broody hen over a sick chick, of a doctor examining her pulse and giving her injections and of Carlos sometimes standing by the bed looking down at her, sometimes sitting in a chair beside the bed, but always watching her with coal-black, expressionless eyes.

Once the fever had left her she had recovered fairly quickly, bouncing back with the resilience of youth, and three days ago she had returned to stay in the bungalow, ostensibly to take up her duties as a wife. But she had seen less of Carlos here than she had seen of him while she had been convalescing at the ranch house. He rose at sunrise and left the house before she got up. Sometimes she saw him at midday, if she was over at the house for lunch, but there was little chance of talking with him about their relationship when his mother was present, and in the evenings after supper he always seemed to have something to do with the administration side of managing the ranch, or he would get in his car and drive away somewhere, only returning after Daphne had gone to bed. She was beginning to feel like a neglected wife.

Her mouth twisted into a wry smile. Why should she worry? She was being paid to sit around like this. Paid to do nothing except appear occasionally to nod and smile at the ranch-hands, to do Teresa's hair and listen to the woman chatter about the past and the Valdez family, to be introduced as Carlos's wife when members of that family called in to visit Teresa. It was easy, too easy, now that Ana-Maria had gone, and she was beginning to get restless and wonder how long Carlos expected her to keep up the masquerade.

Booted feet clumped on the verandah and she glanced at her watch. It was only five-thirty. Carlos was returning early. Her heart seemed to skip a beat and her cheeks grew warm as they always did when she knew he was coming. Picking up the book, she held it in front of her, pretending to read, pretending indifference to his coming even though her nerves were tensing and quivering.

The outer screen door was swung back, the inner door which opened directly into the living room was thrust open. Carlos, wearing a long yellow slicker, a cape-like waterproof which hung from his shoulders and was sleeveless, stepped inside and pushed the door closed. He took off his wet sombrero and shook raindrops from it, pulled the slicker off over his head and hung them both on a hook on the back of the door. Then, turning, he went through to the kitchen without so much as a glance at her.

Her lips tightening as she tried to keep control over an urge to fling down the book and bound to her feet to rush into the kitchen and welcome him, Daphne looked down at the printed page before her. The words danced before her eyes. She couldn't go on like this much longer, she thought desperately, sharing this house with him but wanting to share much more; wanting to share thoughts and dreams with him; wanting to share a bed with him again—he had slept in the loft every night since she had come back to the bungalow; wanting to be his real wife, his love, his mistress.

'*Como esta usted?*'

Slowly she looked up from the book. He had come back into the living room carrying a beer can. While he waited for her answer he ripped the tab off the can and raising it to his lips took a long swig of the beer. He was dressed as usual in his working clothes, the close-fitting grey trousers, the hand-tooled leather riding boots and the loose white Indian shirt made from *manta* or homespun. As always the clothes seemed to enhance the attractions of his lithe, horseman's figure, the graceful length of leg, the leanness of hips, the width of shoulders.

'I feel much better today, thank you,' she said woodenly, and looked down at the book again. To her surprise Carlos sat down beside her on the bamboo settee.

'Do you feel well enough to go into town with me tomorrow?' he asked, leaning back and resting his head against the cushioned back of the settee, stretching his legs out before him. 'I have business to do there with a lawyer and I would like you to be present. You wouldn't have to say anything, just be there.'

'On show as usual, as your wife?' she couldn't help sniping, and turning his head he gave her a slow, inimical glance which made her pulses jump.

'*Si*, as usual, as my wife,' he drawled coolly, and drank more beer. Tilting his head back, he closed his eyes. No longer under the scrutiny of those all-observant black eyes, Daphne laid down her book, and shifting position curled her legs under her on the cushioned seat of the settee, turning sideways so that she could study Carlos's face while he wasn't looking. Beard stubble darkened and blurred the clean line of his jaw and drew attention to the ironic curl of his lips. There were hollows in his cheeks and shadows beneath his eyes and he was frowning as if his thoughts weren't pleasant. Even though he was lying back he was no more relaxed than she was, Daphne thought. He looked tired, and she thought guiltily of the uncomfortable cramped quarters of the loft where he had been sleeping for the past few nights.

'Is the business you have to do with the lawyer connected with Claude Fontaine's will?' she asked.

The thick black lashes flicked up sharply, and the frown deepened. The black eyes stared at her narrowly.

'What do you know of Claude's will?' he demanded. 'Has my mother been talking about it?'

'No. She hasn't said a word about it. Ana-Maria told me.'

'What did she tell you?' he rapped.

'Everything. About how, when she knew Claude Fontaine was going to leave the ranch and half his fortune to you, she persuaded him to add a condition, that you would only inherit if you were married before six months had passed after his death.'

Watching her, he drank the rest of the beer in the can, then put the can down on the floor beside the settee.

'So?' he drawled coolly. 'What else did she tell you?'

'She said you were supposed to marry her but that Claude Fontaine had forgotten to insert her name. Why didn't you wait for her divorce to come through and then marry her?'

'I wanted to inherit the ranch and I couldn't be sure her divorce would be through in time,' he replied smoothly.

'She said you tricked her. You encouraged her to get a divorce so she could marry you and then you married me instead.'

'Ha!' his laugh was short and bitter. 'She didn't need encouraging to get a divorce. She had already filed for one before Claude died. But Miguel Garcia, her husband, wouldn't agree to the settlement she wanted and the proceedings dragged out.'

'But would you have married her if her divorce had come through sooner,' Daphne persisted.

'Only as a last resort to get what I wanted,' he drawled, his mouth twisting cynically. 'Only if I couldn't find someone else to marry.' He gave her a strangely sultry glance. 'I found you and was saved from a fate worse than death—marriage to Ana-Maria,' he said mockingly. 'There was never any love lost between her and me.'

'She told me you and she had always been very close. Like that, she said.' Daphne held up two crossed fingers and his eyebrows tilted satirically.

'That was to make you feel uncomfortable; to make you believe you had come between two lovers by marrying me. She was hoping you would take offence and leave, break up our marriage before I had a chance to show the lawyer that I had carried out the terms of Claude's will.' He glanced away at the rain streaming down the windowpane, his expression grim. 'I knew she could be vindictive, guessed she would try to be revenged on me for not marrying her, but I didn't think she would try to get at me through you.' His glance swerved back to her. 'You shouldn't have gone riding with her that day. You didn't know enough about horses or riding to go that far. My mother tells me you'd only had two lessons.'

'Ana-Maria said you had asked her to teach me to ride so that I could go with you next time you went riding the range, and I've always wanted to learn to ride.' She looked down at her hands which were linked loosely together on her knee. 'And I didn't like to refuse her offer to teach me in case . . . in case she thought I wasn't behaving like a newly married wife usually does; in case she thought I didn't want to please you,' she explained. She raised her eyes and looked at him. 'It was all part of the masquerade,' she added quickly.

'She lied to you,' he said. 'I didn't ask her to teach you to ride. It was her own idea.' He sat up suddenly and leaned forward, thrusting a hand through his already dishevelled hair, then leaning his elbows on his knees, propping his chin on his fists. All Daphne could see of him was the hunch of his shoulders, the way his hair waved down the back of his head and coiled thickly at the nape of his neck. 'It was her idea to mount you on that stubborn little bitch, Black Velvet, too, not mine,' he growled. 'Her idea to take you riding along a dangerous path and to leave you without water. *Dios,* you could have died out there on the range if you hadn't been found that night, don't you realise it?' His voice shook slightly.

'And that would have been on your conscience, wouldn't it?' she couldn't help jibing, and he turned to stare at her, his eyes narrow. 'You brought me here, then you went off and left me here with two strange women. How was I to know Ana-Maria is vindictive and tells lies? How was I to know she hated you and would do anything to be revenged on you? You didn't warn me about her and you didn't tell me why you needed a temporary wife. If I'd known what I know now I'd have been more wary of Ana-Maria.'

'My mother tried to warn you,' he retorted. 'She says she asked you not to go riding so far in the heat of the day, but you ignored her warnings and went anyway. You behaved foolishly and impulsively—God knows why.'

'Perhaps because I am foolish and impulsive,' she said shakily. 'If ... if ... I wasn't I wouldn't be here, would I? I wouldn't have agreed to marry a stranger who wouldn't tell me why he had to have a temporary wife.' She drew a shaky breath and went on more quietly, 'I went riding with Ana-Maria because she said we would ride to meet you.'

'Another of her lies,' he growled. 'She knew I would be returning in exactly the opposite direction. And she lied again when I asked her that evening where you were. She said you'd stayed at the excavation site and would be back the next day. She wanted to stop me from going out to look for you. I didn't believe her and was just setting out when the truck arrived.' Again his laugh was short and bitter. 'It didn't take long for Ana-Maria to get the message that she wouldn't be welcome here any more. She left the same night.'

'Where did she go?' asked Daphne.

'I don't know and I don't care, but I'm pretty sure she'll never come back,' he replied harshly.

'Not even for the settlement of the will, to receive her portion of Claude Fontaine's fortune?'

He half-turned to look at her again, one eyebrow raised in mocking surprise.

'What fortune?' he said scoffingly. 'Claude didn't have a fortune, when he died.' He shook his head and laughed a little. 'Poor Claude! He was the last of the Fontaines, as decadent as they come because the family was inbred. He was pleasant enough and well educated, but weak, and the money he had inherited put him at the mercy of a certain sort of women; a woman like Ana-Maria's mother, Maria Fontaine, his own cousin. She persuaded him to marry her when she found herself pregnant by another man then rooked his fortune from him in a divorce settlement. All he had left was the ranch, and that was in a bad way.'

'Until your mother had the idea of asking you to come and manage it and then persuaded him to leave it to you. Doesn't she belong to the group of a certain sort of women you referred to, as well? Wasn't Claude at her mercy too?' Daphne challenged him. 'Oh, I think none of you are very nice people. You're all avaricious and grasping for something that belongs to someone else.' she exclaimed, her voice choking a little.

'I guessed you wouldn't understand,' Carlos said quietly. 'That's why I didn't tell you why I needed to get married. You're from a different country and a different culture, so I couldn't expect you to understand this passion for the land which my mother has, passed on to her from her father. José is like that too. All the Valdez family are, even I.' He paused, then went on softly, 'In wanting to acquire the Fontaine ranch we haven't been grasping for something that doesn't belong to us. The land is ours and tomorrow, in spite of Ana-Maria's trick to try and prevent it from happening, the lawyer will hand over the original grant made to the Fontaine family to me when I show the proof of my marriage to you. Then the land will be redeveloped into an *ejido* based on cattle raising and each one of us will have a share in its success.' He turned to her again. 'Do you understand now?'

'I'm trying to,' she sighed. 'But do you think Claude Fontaine really forgot to put Ana-Maria's name in the condition he added to his will?'

'We'll never know, will we?' he shrugged. 'But thank God it wasn't put in.' He made as if to rise to his feet. 'So you will go to bed early and get up early to go with me to the town?' he said abruptly.

'Yes, I will. Where are you going now?'

'To the village.'

'Oh, please don't go.' she said urgently, reaching out to place a hand on his arm. 'Stay here with me. It's so lonely when you're not here. Stay with me, or take me with you to where you go when you go out, where you went last night and the night before.'

Under her fingers his arm tensed, he turned his head and looked down at her hand, then gave her an up-from-under glance which made her pulses leap, and she withdrew her hand hurriedly.

'I warned you not to pull that trick again,' he said tersely.

'And I told you that it isn't a trick,' she whispered. 'Please don't go out without me. Take me with you.'

'To the *cantina*, in the village?' he said softly. 'No way. I'm not having all the men down there making eyes at you.'

'Then stay here with me, please.' Her cheeks were flaming suddenly and she couldn't look at him. Never would she have believed she could lower her pride so much as to plead with a man to stay with her, but here she was doing it because she didn't want to spend the night alone.

Carlos's fingertips were rough against her skin as they tilted her chin up, forcing her to look at him. In the greyish gloom of the room his eyes glittered like pieces of jet as they searched her face while his fingers slid gently along her jaw to curve about her neck. Slowly his lips approached hers.

Warm, sensually soft, tasting slightly of the beer he had drunk, his lips teased hers, seducing them into parting. Against the skin at the nape of her neck his fingers stroked delicately, sending delicious shivers down her spine. Released by his touch, the feelings she had been holding in check surged through her freely, and her arms went round him. Her fingers revelled in the thickness of his hair. With a sigh of pleasure she leaned against him, and together they subsided sideways against the back of the settee.

Outside the rain continued to fall. Inside the shadows deepened and lengthened, but neither of them noticed as their kisses became hungrier and deeper, their hands took more liberties until they were both breathless and dizzy with desire, teetering on the edge of consummation.

Carlos drew back from the edge first, his hands on her shoulders pushing her away from him so that he could look at her. Heavy-lidded, his eyes still smouldered with passion and his lips still curved sensually.

'Making love isn't in the deal we made with each other,' he murmured.

'I know.' Daphne's lips were throbbing and every part of her that he had touched was tingling and aching to be touched again and released from the agony of desire. 'But that doesn't mean we shouldn't make love if we want to,' she whispered.

She slid her hand within the opening of his shirt again, having discovered the delight of touching him. The hairs on his chest were crisp and tickled the palm of her hand. The skin of his shoulder was as smooth as silk. He smelt of horses, sweat and beer, and once she would have withdrawn from such intimate contact, would have been revolted by the heady, earthy aroma. But on Carlos's sun-bronzed skin and hair the tangy scents only seemed to enhance his masculine potency. They excited her, and she longed to be swept against him again and to feel the heat of his mouth on hers. Slowly she lifted her lips to his in silent seduction.

But his lips didn't touch hers again. Drawing in his breath with a savage hiss, he tipped his head back out of her reach and shoving her away from him sprang to his feet, turning away from the settee to stride over to the window and stand with his back to her, his hands thrust into his trouser pockets his shoulders hunched.

'What's the matter?' Daphne cried, scrambling off the settee and going after him. 'Didn't you like what we were doing?'

He swung round to face her, bone ridged white along the angle of his jaw as he exerted control.

'What do you think?' he jeered. 'I'm a man, aren't I, with hot blood in my veins. I like to make love to a woman and lie with her. I'd like to make love to you and lie with you on that bed in there.' He gestured towards the passage which led to the bedroom. 'But it wasn't in the bargain we struck, and I'm not going to let you throw away your virginity just because you're trapped in marriage to me.'

'But I want to make love with you and go all the way. Oh, Carlos, don't you see. . . .'

'No!' He spoke violently and his eyes flashed. 'Don't *you* see that you're playing with fire? If we did what you want, if we went all the way, you'd only regret it later, and we wouldn't be able to have the marriage annulled easily. Ah, *Dios*, don't look like that, *querida!*' His arms were around her suddenly and she was crushed against his chest as he tried to comfort her. 'Don't you think I have enough on my conscience without having that too? I shouldn't have asked you to marry me. I shouldn't have brought you here, but I thought you were tougher than you are, were less innocent than you are.' He pushed her away from him again. 'In two weeks it will all be over,' he went on quietly, his dark eyes steady on hers. 'I'll take you to Mexico City and put you on a plane for London. Once you're in your own country you'll soon forget and be glad we didn't go all the way.'

There was no softening in his attitude. He was tougher than she was and more able to resist temptation because he was older and more experienced—but most of all because he wasn't in love with her. Her shoulders slumped and she wandered listlessly back to the lounger. Flopping down on it, she picked up the book. Behind her she heard the thud of Carlos's boots as he crossed the room, followed by the rustle of his slicker as he took it down and slipped it on. In a few seconds he had gone and the only sound was the perpetual drumming of rain on the roof.

Later that evening, unable to stand being alone any longer, Daphne pulled on a spare slicker and tying a scarf over her head made her way across the muddy yard to the big house to spend the evening with Teresa. It wasn't unusual, she had found, for the young wife to spend time with her mother-in-law in that part of the world. It showed she had respect for her husband's mother and was not averse to keeping the elderly woman company.

Not that Teresa lacked company. Several members of the Valdez family were visiting her, two cousins and their wives as well as José Valdez and his wife. They were all seated round the dining room table playing cards, a game called *canasta*, and after welcoming Daphne they insisted that she join them even though she couldn't speak the language and would have to depend on Teresa to translate anything any of them said to her.

Although she remained mystified as to what the game was about she enjoyed the evening and helped Teresa to serve coffee and cakes afterwards. Everyone seemed friendly towards her and all the women kissed her soundly on the cheeks when they left. After helping Teresa to wash up and put away she said goodnight and returned to the bungalow, sloshing through mud, hoping to see Carlos' car parked outside and a light glowing from within the house, hoping he was back so that she could talk to him again and perhaps persuade him to sleep with her.

But there was no car and no light, even though it was almost midnight. In a bedroom which felt damp, Daphne got into a bed which felt even damper and switched off the light, knowing that she wouldn't sleep until she heard the car and saw the beam of its headlights swerve past the window.

It came at last, and she lay tense and alert, list-

ening to the doors open and close, seeing light
slant across the passage beyond the open bedroom
door, hearing the bathroom door open and close,
then open and close again a few minutes later.
Then silence. Then the unmistakable creak of leather boots as someone walked very quietly towards
the bedroom. When she saw his shape loom in
the doorway she spoke.

'Carlos?'

'Hmm? Why aren't you asleep?' he whispered.

'I was waiting to hear you come in. What have
you been doing at the *cantina*?'

'Drinking *tequila*.' He sounded amused.

'Oh. Why?'

'To get drunk.'

'Oh! How unpleasant. Are you drunk?' She
lunged up on the bed and peered towards the
doorway.

'No, but I'm not sober either.' Mockery rippled
through his voice again.

'Are you going to sleep in here, with me?' she
whispered.

'No.'

'Then why did you come?'

'To make sure you are still here. I wouldn't
like you to be missing in the morning when I go
to the lawyer's office. He'll want to meet you as
well as see the proof of our marriage. *Buenas
noches, querida.*'

'I wish you'd tell me what *querida* means,' she
said crossly, but he'd gone and she couldn't even
hear his boots creaking as he walked along the
passage.

Daphne was tempted to follow him, but pride stepped in suddenly as she remembered the way he had rejected her that afternoon. She wasn't going to risk rejection a third time. Carlos must have sensed that he had hurt her, though, or he wouldn't have taken her in his arms to comfort her afterwards. And he wouldn't have come to the bedroom now to check on whether she was still here. He'd been worried in case she had left before he had been able to introduce her to the lawyer.

But how could she leave when she had no means of transport to the nearest town, when she was dependent on him to go anywhere? Two weeks more, he had said, and then it would be all over. Oh, God she wouldn't be able to stand another two weeks of being near him and living with him in every way except one. She would have to leave. Why couldn't she leave as soon as they had seen the lawyer, as soon as Carlos had got what he wanted, the title deed to the ranch? Why prolong the agony?

She would ask him tomorrow morning if she could leave and go to Mexico City tomorrow afternoon or the next day. He didn't have to go with her and see her on to the plane for London. There must be buses going from Micatepec to the capital, and once there she would be able to find her way to the International Airport.

She must leave while she still had a certain amount of control over her feelings; before she was overwhelmed by the whirlpool of sexual passion in which she seemed to have been caught. She must get away from the handsome, complex, tantalisingly enigmatic Carlos before he dominated her completely.

He wakened her at sunrise by banging on the bedroom door with the flat of his hand. In the small kitchen they drank the coffee he had made and ate *tortillas* wrapped round scrambled eggs with slices of beef jerky or *machacado*. Not yet dressed, Daphne wore a thin flowered kimono-styled wrap over her nightdress. But Carlos was almost formally dressed in the suit he had worn when she had first met him, with a clean crisp cream shirt, open at the collar. Freshly shaved and washed, he was as uncommunicative as ever, not even looking at her as he ate quickly, rising from the table as soon as he had finished to carry his plate and mug over to the sink.

Hearing Bonita entering the house, Daphne spoke quickly before the housemaid could enter the kitchen.

'I've been thinking,' she began, then added urgently as he ignored her and went towards the door of the kitchen, 'Carlos, wait! There's something I must ask you.'

'So? Ask me in the car on the way to the town. I'm going over to the house now to see if my mother is ready.' His dark glance flicked over her impersonally. 'I would be glad if you would hurry, *por favor*,' he added coolly. 'We must be at the lawyer's office before ten. That is the deadline.'

'But in the car will be too late,' she cried,

springing up from the table and going after him, colliding with Bonita as the girl entered the kitchen with her bucket and mop. 'I must know now. Carlos, please wait for a moment.' Breathlessly she caught up with him at the front door. 'I can't ask you in front of your mother . . . because I don't know how much she knows . . . about us,' she added.

'She knows nothing,' he replied coldly. 'She thinks you are the woman I went to meet and marry in Acapulco, that's all. What do you want to know?'

'I wondered . . . since you'll have got what you want today and will have proved that you're married to the lawyer if . . . if I could leave this afternoon or tomorrow.' Daphne paused, finding her throat suddenly closing up. In spite of her resolve not to touch him her hand went out to play with the lapel of his jacket. 'I . . . I . . . don't think I can bear living with you for another two weeks without . . . without making demands that you don't like.' Her voice trailed away weakly.

Under her hand his chest rose and fell as he drew in a sharp breath. He raised a hand and caught hold of hers, and for a moment they stared at each other. His mouth was taut, his cheeks hollow, his eyes deeply shadowed, and she guessed he hadn't slept any more than she had and was possibly suffering from the after-effects of too much *tequila*.

'You must leave if you wish, of course,' he said slowly, lifting her hand from his jacket and dropping it suddenly as if he had received a shock from it. 'But you'll go without the money I promised to pay you. I won't have it to give to you until the fourteenth of May, about two weeks from now. But if you want to go today I won't stop you. I have no right to.'

'Thank you.' The words came out as the merest whisper as she stepped back from him. For a few seconds they stood staring at each other and it seemed to Daphne that in spite of the humidity the air between them was static with tension and she knew instinctively that neither of them was saying what they wanted to say. They were lying to each other, putting on an act, hiding from a violent, passionate attraction to each other that threatened to change their lives completely.

Suddenly Carlos turned away and went out through the front door. It crashed closed after him and Daphne stood listening to his booted feet clumping across the verandah before he leapt down the steps into the yard. Vaguely she heard the clatter Bonita was making in the kitchen and the voice of one of the ranch hands calling to Carlos as he crossed the yard.

She could go if *she* wished. He was taking no responsibility for her leaving. Well, she had an answer to her request, so what was she waiting for? Whirling round, she ran into the bedroom and dressed quickly in a short white linen skirt and shocking-pink short-sleeved V-necked cotton top. Finding her suitcase, she dragged it out and began to fling clothing into it. When it was full she locked it, then checked that she had her passport and money in her shoulder bag. Then picking up the suitcase, she lugged it through the living room and out of the house. She had just reached the car when Carlos returned. He took one look at her case and unlocked the boot of the car without a word and heaved the case into it. There was no time for her to say anything to him because Teresa appeared around the corner of the barn, smartly dressed in a pleated black skirt and short-sleeved white blouse, a dark coloured *rebozo* or stole around her shoulders.

Although the rain had stopped thick grey clouds still covered the sky and the air was heavy and humid. As the car rolled along the dirt road to the Highway huge waves of water surged up around it whenever it passed through one of the big puddles, and there were times when Daphne thought the whole vehicle would be engulfed by the water. In the distance the foothills had almost disappeared in a grey haze and the flat range land looked even more desolate than when she had first seen it the evening she had come with Carlos.

Her glance swerved from the land to Carlos. In the back seat of the car she was sitting directly behind him. Teresa sat beside him, chattering volubly as usual, not seeming to mind that she never received an answer from the taciturn man who was her son. Daphne's glance lingered on his thick tawny hair and on the broad slope of his shoulders. Her hands gripped each other in her lap as she restrained a desire to reach out and ruffle his hair, slide her arms forward over his shoulders, rub her cheek against his.

They reached the Highway and turned on to it.

There was not much traffic and the miles flashed by. Soon they were in the outskirts of the town, driving past flat-roofed modern apartment buildings. By the time they reached the centre of the town the sun was beginning to peep through the clouds to glint on the tiled roofs of the old French houses. Two and sometimes three storeys high, often with dormer windows in their steeply sloped roofs, each of their long windows flanked by wooden shutters, they were very similar to houses in the villages and towns of northern France and were quite unrelated to the Spanish Colonial style with its high white walls, curving arches and wrought-iron grilles and gateways. Tall elegant pillars supported the high roofs of verandahs that shaded windows and doorways from the sun and leafy vines climbed everywhere, the purple red blossoms of bougainvillea foaming over trellises and walls.

As in most developing Mexican towns there was a modern part consisting of oblongs and squares of concrete and glass, and it was in one of the new high-rise buildings that the lawyer's office was situated. While Carlos and Teresa met the lawyer in his inner sanctum Daphne sat in the secretary's office leafing through a magazine. After a while Carlos came out of the inner office and beckoned to her. She went with him and was introduced to the lawyer. Punctiliously polite, the lawyer took her hand and raised it to his lips to kiss the back of it in the Latin fashion, saluting her as he would have saluted any married women.

She didn't have to say anything other than,

'*Buenos dias,*' and soon she was leaving the office building with Carlos and Teresa, stepping out into hot hazy sunshine.

'So now you and I go shopping, Daphne,' said Teresa authoritatively when they were seated in the car again. 'Carlos will drive us to the farmers' market and leave us there while he goes to the bank and visits the stock market. Where will we meet you for lunch, Carlos?'

'At Angelo's, the seafood restaurant on the *zocalo*. I'll leave the car parked there and we can wait for each other there. About twelve-thirty?'

'*Si*. That will be good.' Teresa turned and beamed at Daphne over the back seat. It was obvious the woman was well-satisfied with what had happened in the lawyer's office. 'We will celebrate,' she said. 'Your marriage and Carlos's inheritance of the Fontaine ranch.' Her black eyes flashed with passionate feelings. 'I cannot tell you how glad I am that at last the land has been returned to our people,' she said fiercely. 'My father must be singing in heaven to know that his ambition has been achieved.' She glanced sideways at Daphne again, her disarming smile crinkling the corners of her eyes and showing her white teeth. 'You think I am a little *loca*, touched in the head, perhaps,' she pointed a forefinger at her temple and jiggled it about, 'to go on in this way?' she added.

'I think you are no different from any other person who loves their country as well as freedom,' replied Daphne gently. 'And I'm sure that without people like you and your father Mexico would still be ruled by absentee landowners and dictators.'

'Aha, Carlos has been teaching you well,' said Teresa, nodding with pleasure. 'It is true we have needed revolutions in the past. But now we need people like my Juan—God rest his soul—and like Carlos, people with skills and know-how to help us use our land properly and to develop it; people who can build industries and teach us how to work in them. People like you, too, Daphne.' Teresa's eyes twinkled with affection. 'And yours and Carlos's children.'

'I hope so,' Daphne muttered, and sank back in her seat. She was glad they had reached the square with its neat flower beds ablaze with marigolds and zinnias and its shady trees. Carlos parked the car in front of the restaurant and they all got out. He walked off in one direction and she and Teresa walked in another, down a narrow street towards the market.

Farmers had brought their produce to sell and had spread their wares out along several narrow streets under white canvas awnings. As she wandered from one stall to the next admiring the pyramids of fresh fruit and the huge bunches of colourful flowers Daphne lagged slowly behind Teresa, intending to go back to the square where she had noticed a boutique selling women's clothing. She wanted to buy a small gift for Teresa as a token of her appreciation of the woman's careful nursing of her when she had been ill.

As soon as she saw Teresa involved in haggling about the price of some oranges with the proprietor of a fruit stall she turned quickly and hurried back the way she had come, dodging around people and baskets of fruit and vegetables. At last she reached the end of the narrow street. There was no sign of Teresa, so she hurried towards the square.

Soon she was in the boutique admiring the embroidered *huipils*, rectangular traditional Indian dresses, all made from different coloured cottons, some simply embroidered around the neck and the hem, others heavily decorated with ribbons and bands of colour. There were also *quechquemitls*, triangular garments made from two pieces of cloth, the short side of each piece sewn to the long side of the other with an opening for the neck, which she had seen women on the ranch wearing over their blouses.

Some headdresses on show were merely scarves or satin ribbons to weave into the hair, but some were magnificent lace *mantillas*. And there was jewellery, strings and strings of coloured glass beads, coral and silver necklaces with pendant triple crosses and earrings also made from beads.

After some serious consideration of price and style she chose a *quechquemitl* for Teresa. Made from dark red cotton, it was hand-embroidered in black and white in an Indian design. With her purchase wrapped in soft white paper she stepped into the street again and looked round for a policeman to ask the way to the bus station.

'Hey, Daphne—Daphne Thomas Reynolds! It is you, isn't it?'

The voice which called to her was young and

male, vaguely familiar. She glanced over her shoulder. A tall young man dressed in blue jeans and a blue T-shirt, a straw sombrero tilted rakishly on his head, was striding towards her.

'Don't you remember me?' he queried, coming to a stop in front of her. 'I'm the guy who picked you up off the ground just over a week ago, out on the ranch. Tom Hutton is the name. How are you?'

CHAPTER SEVEN

DAPHNE stared up at the brown-bearded face, the blue eyes, and for a few seconds was in darkness, in the front of the truck, being held by strong arms and comforted by a light, slightly mocking voice.

'Yes, I remember,' she said, smiling up at him spontaneously and shaking his outstretched hand. 'Are you still working at the excavation site?'

'Afraid not. We packed up yesterday,' he replied. 'The weather's becoming unsuitable for digging, too wet and muggy. Dig ... that's Diego Gutierrez, and I call him Dig for short,' his sudden grin was bright and merry, mocking himself, 'well, he and I are on our way back to Mexico City. I don't know whether I told you, but we're both studying at the Institute of Anthropology and History and we were brought down here by one of the professors to help with the excavation.'

'I don't know whether you told me or not, either,' she said. 'I'm afraid I wasn't all there when you found me. But I'm glad you noticed me and spoke to me just now. I've been wanting to thank you for what you did that night. If you hadn't found me. . . .' She broke off, shuddering.

'You'd have become vulture meat,' he said, his grin becoming macabre. 'I called in at the ranch a few days later to ask how you were, and your husband told me you were making progress.' He slanted a vivid blue glance down at her, his expression curious. 'He thanked me on your behalf, but he wasn't very friendly and wouldn't let me see you. Did he tell you I'd called to see you?'

'No, he didn't.' Daphne frowned slightly, wondering why Carlos hadn't told her. Surely he must have known she would have liked a visit from this pleasant, cheerful young man.

'I've thought about you a lot since then, couldn't help wondering how a nice girl from Wales like you got entangled with a tough guy like him and ended up on a ranch in the state of Veracruz. How come you're such a long way from home?'

'It's a long story,' she murmured evasively, avoiding his eyes. 'You wouldn't know where the bus station is, would you?'

'Sure, I know. I'll drive you over there if you like. It's a goodish walk from here, in the new section of town. The truck is parked on the other side of the square. Come on, let's cross now while there's no traffic.'

He put a hand under her elbow and they hurried across the street to the centre of the square and walked along a diagonal path through the flowerbeds to the red and cream Ford pick-up truck which was parked at the kerbside.

'Dig is saying goodbye to his girl-friend,' explained Tom Hutton once they were in the truck and it was moving forward. He flashed a grin in Daphne's direction. 'He comes from around here. I guess he'll be some time. She's quite a doll, lives in one of those old French houses.' He glanced at her curiously again. 'Why do you want to go to the bus station?' he asked. 'Are you planning on going somewhere?'

'Yes. I'd like to get to Mexico City today,' she replied coolly.

He made no comment, being busy guiding the truck down a very narrow cobble-stoned street. At the end of the street was the modern part of the town, and after a while he turned off a wide roadway into the parking lot of a shopping mall.

'The bus station is right here,' he said, turning off the truck's engine. 'The office is in the shopping mall. Like me to come with you?'

'Would you mind? I can't speak much Spanish and I can never understand when anyone speaks to me in the language. They always speak so fast.'

In the busy office she told him what she wanted to know and he asked the clerk in fairly fluent Spanish, then translated the answers back to her. It appeared that she would have to go by bus to

Tuxpan and change there on to another bus going to the capital.

'I guess you're not going to make it today,' said Tom. 'The bus to Tuxpan has just left and there won't be another until late this afternoon. You'd have to stay the night in Tuxpan and catch the first bus to the capital tomorrow. Or alternatively stay the night in town here and then catch the first bus to Tuxpan from here. It'll take you about ten hours in all, three to Tuxpan, seven from there to Mexico City. What are you going to do?'

'I . . . I'm not sure,' she murmured. 'I'll have to think.'

'Well, while you're thinking come and have a cup of coffee,' said the cheerful Tom. 'There's a café right over there.'

They sat in a corner booth where there was only room for two and were waited on by a dark-faced Indian boy. For a while there was silence between them. Daphne was busy trying to decide what to do, whether to go back to the ranch with Carlos and Teresa, grit her teeth and stay the two weeks until Carlos had the money to pay her, or whether to take the next bus to Tuxpan, stay the night there and catch the first bus to Mexico City in the morning.

'Going to tell me that long story?' asked Tom, his voice jolting her out of her thoughts. She looked up. He wasn't much older than herself and with his brown hair and blue eyes he could pass for her brother. Although they weren't related she felt he was kin to her, a familiar friendly person among strangers whom she could trust and who had already helped her. Could she trust him with her story? She felt she could, and she began to tell it to him.

She told him everything, from the moment she had collided with Carlos at Elsa's party to the moment at the bungalow when she had told Carlos she wouldn't be able to stay for another two weeks. She left out only the intimate details. Tom listened intently, the expressions on his face ranging from scepticism through astonishment to final irritation and anger.

'My God, he's got a nerve!' he exclaimed when she had finished. 'Offering to pay you to be his wife for a while and then going back on his word. If I were you I'd hang on, get that money he promised. You know, I guessed there was something fishy about the set-up when I found you out of your mind with fever lying in the middle of a dirt road crossing one of the biggest ranches in the region. Then Reynolds was so damned cool and offhand when I called to ask about you, as if he didn't want me to know you. But you can't leave him yet. You've got to hang in there for the money. You've done a lot for him one way and another, and you've earned it.'

'But I don't think I can stay,' she whispered. 'I can't stay any longer.'

'No?' Tom's eyebrows went up. He stared at her, his eyes narrowing slowly, a knowledgeable gleam glinting in them. 'Ah, so that's it,' he said. 'A bit of a brute, is he? Been taking advantage of the situation.'

'Oh, no,' said Daphne quickly, 'he hasn't. We . . . I . . . well, he offered me the position of being his temporary wife to help me because I didn't have much money. He had to get married so he could get control of the ranch to develop it as an *ejido*. He's really a very fine person who cares about other people.'

'Oh, yeah?' jeered Tom. 'You're sure of that?'

'Yes, I'm sure. If he hadn't inherited the ranch it would have gone to that scheming gold-digger Ana-Maria Fontaine and then nobody would have had a share in it,' she retorted.

'Okay, okay,' said Tom. 'I get the picture. In spite of the fact that he's gone back on his word to you, you like him, admire and respect him, but you just can't handle being his temporary wife. Right?'

'Right,' she muttered. As she had guessed, he was kin to her. He understood the way she felt about Carlos without her having to go into details. 'I thought I could do it and come through untouched,' she said. 'I thought I could play the part without becoming emotionally involved. But I couldn't, and now I have to leave while I can ... before I lose the ability to act independently and before he's able to raise the money to pay me. That's why I want to go to Mexico City. I thought I might be able to get a job there.'

'Doing what?'

'Hairdressing. I'm qualified.'

'How much money do you have?'

'Not much,' she admitted, thinking guiltily of the cost of the gift she had bought for Teresa. 'About seven hundred *pesos*.'

'Whew!' Tom's whistle was derisive. 'That isn't

going to go far when you reach the capital.' He paused, looking away from her, his eyes narrow and thoughtful. 'You're all ready to go?' he asked at last, looking at her. 'You've got passport and money with you, your other belongings?'

'Yes, I'm all ready to go. I suppose I could catch the afternoon bus to Tuxpan and spend the night in the bus station there to wait for the first bus to Mexico City,' she said.

'I've got a better idea,' he said coolly, putting a hand in his jeans pocket and finding a coin which he tossed on to the table as a tip. 'You can come with Dig and me. There's room in the truck, and when we get to the capital you can stay with us. We share an apartment there.'

'It's very kind of you to offer,' said Daphne hesitantly, 'but I'm not sure if . . . if I should.'

'I am,' he said firmly, and leaned towards her across the table, his blue eyes earnest and serious. 'If you really want to get out of the emotional involvement you've got yourself into you'll come with us. It's your best chance. You need help with the lingo and you don't have much money. I can help you with both because I can speak Spanish, I have a vehicle in which you can ride and I have somewhere you can stay while you try to find a job. If you pass up such a good offer, God knows what will happen to you. You'll get on the wrong bus or something. Or some other guy less quixotic than I,' his brash grin flashed out mocking himself again, 'will take advantage of you. Like Carlos Reynolds did.'

'He didn't!' Daphne retorted furiously. 'I went

into the arrangement with my eyes wide open. I
knew what I was doing when I agreed to marry him.
It was the only way I could save him from being put
in prison on a false charge of kidnapping.'

'All right, keep your hair on,' Tom mocked.
'Are you going to come with Dig and me?'

'Yes, please,' she whispered miserably. 'But
you'll have to take me back to the square. My
suitcase is in the back of Carlos's car. I'll have to
find him to get it and to tell him I'm leaving with
you. I'm supposed to meet him and his mother
for lunch at Angelo's at twelve-thirty.'

'Okay, we'll go right there,' said Tom, rising to
his feet. 'It's twenty after twelve now.'

To her relief Carlos was by the car, leaning
against it lazily, talking to another man in range
clothes, when Daphne crossed the square from
the place where Tom had parked it. As soon as he
saw her, Carlos straightened up and said something to the other man, who walked off with a
wave of his hand. There was no sign of Teresa.

'I guess you've lost my mother,' said Carlos,
his mouth curving into a sardonic smile. 'It was
inevitable. She loves to bargain in the market.
She'll turn up sooner or later. Would you like to
go into the restaurant and we'll have a drink
before eating?'

'No. No, thanks,' she said breathlessly. 'I . . .
I'd like my case, please. I . . . I've got a lift to
Mexico City. I'm going with Tom Hutton and
his friend Diego.'

She couldn't be sure because his face was
shaded by the brim of his sombrero, but she

thought he went a little pale. He didn't move and for a wild, hopeful moment she thought he was going to refuse to let her have her case, possibly entreat her not to leave yet and return to the ranch with him. Then he shrugged and taking out his keys stepped round to the back of the car, unlocked it and took out her case. He set it down beside her.

'You didn't lose much time in finding another protector,' he drawled, and every word stung her like the steel tip of a whip might, but she didn't retort. Her lips trembling slightly, she held out the parcel containing Teresa's gift to him.

'Please give this to your mother ... with my love,' she muttered, and watched his brown hand reach out to take it from her. 'And explain to her.'

'Sure I'll explain. I'll tell her you've left me for another man,' said Carlos, and her glance flew upwards to his face. The black eyes were glinting with bitter mockery, the long mouth was curved downwards at the corners.

'Oh, no, don't,' she pleaded. 'She'll think so badly of me if you do.'

'But I'd only be telling her the truth, wouldn't I?' he taunted. 'You are going with another man.'

'But not because I prefer him to you,' she argued urgently. 'I'm going with Tom because it's convenient and you know you don't want me to stay with you any longer than necessary. You don't need a masquerade wife any more—you've got what you wanted. Goodbye, Carlos.' She held out her hand to him.

He didn't take her hand but looked at her with

blank cold eyes as if he couldn't see her. She
picked up her case and began to move away, ready
to cross the street to the truck. Behind her Carlos
said softly,

'*Adios, querida.* Let me know how you go on in
the capital. Send me an address so that I can mail
the money to you.'

'I don't want the money!' she cried in a stifled
voice, and stepped to the edge of the sidewalk.
'Please don't send it to me. I don't want it.'

She didn't look at him again but plunged across
the street, never realising that she forced a car to
come to an abrupt stop with a screech of tyres.
Tom took her case from her and put it in the
back of the truck, then opened the door so that
she could climb up on to the bench seat to sit
between him and Diego.

Handsome in a Latin way, with olive skin and
black curly hair, Diego greeted her politely and
asked after her health, then turned on the truck
engine and put it into gear. As it trundled down
the street Daphne looked back through the windscreen behind her, just in time to see Teresa
arriving at Angelo's, her shopping basket laden.

At first Tom and Diego talked to her, telling her
about themselves, almost as if both of them
guessed she was feeling sad, as if a little of her
had died when she had parted from Carlos and
soon she learned that they were both taking post-
graduate degrees in anthropology at the Institute
and were fascinated by the origins of the
American Indians (so-called), having particular

interest, of course, in those of Mexico—the Aztecs, the Mayas and before them the Olmecs and the Zapotecs, the Mixtec and the Tarascans.

'Man has lived in Mesoamerica, this part of the continent, for about thirty thousand years,' said Tom enthusiastically, 'and has spoken with as many as twelve hundred dialects stemming from a hundred and forty different languages, which indicates that there were many different tribes.'

'What have you been looking for at the site where you've been excavating?' asked Daphne, making an effort to be interested, knowing that only by responding to their kindness would she be able to prevent herself from dwelling despondently on what might have been between Carlos and herself.

'Remains of houses, debris of tools and cooking utensils used long ago,' replied Diego. 'And we've found them. From studying them, we've discovered that the people who lived here as long ago as 2900 B.C. were what we call hunters and gatherers. They used canoes and collected fish, shellfish and fruits as well as hunting game. We've also found some ceramic bowls of a later date, indicating that the place of the hunters and gatherers was taken by a maize-growing people, probably Olmecs, who were later overwhelmed by the Maya-related Huaestecs who built El Tajin.'

'What's that?' asked Daphne.

'It was a city, located in a valley between two major rivers. It dominated the river alluvial plains and controlled trade and became the religious centre for the Totonac Indians who moved into this region and helped Corte's, the Spanish conquistador, to defeat the Aztecs.'

'They're still here, the Totonacs,' said Tom. 'And I wouldn't be at all surprised if your hus ... I mean Carlos Reynolds' mother was part Totonac.'

'She told me her father was Luis Valdez who fought for the Zapatistas in the Revolutionary war,' said Daphne.

'Ah, that explains it,' said Tom. 'The fierce desire to get control of the ranch. Valdez was a *mestizo*, half *criollo*—that means of Spanish blood but born in New Spain—and half Totonac. He believed the land belonged to him and his people and not to the French emigrés who came here to settle and were granted tracts of land.' He slanted a glance at Daphne. 'You've been caught up in a local feud,' he remarked dryly, 'or you could call it a mini-revolution engineered by a formidable matriarch, Señora Teresa Valdez Reynolds de Fontaine ... I hope I have all her surnames in the right order.'

'Maybe we should show Daphne El Tajin,' said Diego as the truck swooped out of Naulta and along the road north to Papantla. 'She may not come this way again.'

'Good thinking,' replied Tom cheerfully. 'I wouldn't mind having a look at the Temple of the Niches again, either, and it won't take us much out of our way. Are you interested, Daphne?'

'Yes, of course.'

Diego's words, spoken in all innocence had plunged her in nostalgia for those few hours she had spent in Taxco with Carlos. *You and I might never come this way again, so we should see all we can while we can,* Carlos had said, and it was then that she had fallen in love with him, she could see that now. She had fallen in love so deeply that she hadn't hesitated an hour or so later to marry him.

Then why hadn't she stayed with him? Why hadn't she hung in there, as Tom had suggested? Was it because she had realised Carlos didn't love her? Or had she been hoping, when she confronted him with the actual fact of her leaving, when she had asked him for her suitcase in Micatepec, that he would have taken some sort of action to stop her from leaving?

Like catching her up in his arms and throwing her across his saddle to gallop off with her to his ranch like a hero in a Wild West film? Her twisted smile mocked herself and her lively romantic imagination. That sort of behaviour belonged to the past, here in Mexico as much as in the United States, if indeed anyone ever had behaved like that. It belonged in romantic stories, and Carlos wasn't at all romantic, he had shown that he wasn't several times. He probably had no time for the emotion described as 'being in love' and had never experienced it, even though he had admitted to 'liking' women and 'liking making love to a woman'.

She would do her best to forget him. She would close the door on her adventure with him and look forward to finding a job in Mexico City. Something would turn up, it always did, and meanwhile she had two new friends to help her.

In another hour the truck was passing through the sleepy little town of Papantla, then turning on to a narrow country road, pitted with potholes, that led to the famous ruins. Soon they were standing before the Temple, a tiered pyramid with a hundred and sixty-five niches or holes set in rows along each tier, and Tom was explaining that it was a shrine dedicated to the rain and the wind, the two deities at the centre of the Tajin religion followed by the Totonacs.

'This temple was probably reserved for the burial of men of high position. Many human sacrifices were made to the gods and death in the ball courts was attended by the ritual drinking of *pulque*, a fermented liquor. El Tajin had at least ten ball courts.'

'Tennis courts, you mean?' asked Daphne, who was beginning to suffer from mental indigestion from having absorbed so much ancient history in such a short time.

'No,' laughed Diego, shaking his head. 'The game was played with a solid rubber ball which was volleyed from one end of the court to the other by use of the hips, perhaps the elbows and upper arms or even the knees. It was a deadly serious game and a player would be chosen to be beheaded at the end of the game. After a while, though, the drinking of *pulque* ritual became more important than the ball game.'

'Why?'

'The idea behind it was to propitiate the rain god by drinking the liquor and evoke visions of life after death and the gods of the underworld. The rain god is also the *pulque* god, because without rain the *maguey* plant from which *pulque* was made wouldn't grow.'

They wandered around the ruins for another hour until light began to fade from the sky. Then they watched, with a group of tourists, a fantastic aerial ballet performed by a team of *voladores*, Totonac Indians who practised a ritual more than a thousand years old.

From the top of a hundred-foot pole *tocatines* (flyers) fell from a simple wooden frame, and when the ropes supporting them had completely unwound they began to fly around the pole to the accompaniment of flute music played by their captain, who sat on a tiny platform at the top of the pole.

Watching the slim figures dance in the air with rare acrobatic skill, listening to the plaintive wail of the flute while shadows crept about the ancient stone pyramids, Daphne felt as if she had been transported back in time to a pagan world of strange beliefs and weird beauty.

But the modern world soon took over again as they left the temple and drove on towards Poza Rica, where steelworks belched forth sulphur fumes and the sky, heavy with clouds, pulsated with colour, glowing red and pink as it reflected the burn-off of gas in the oil-fields to the north.

With the coming of darkness the rest of the drive to the capital was tedious, although they stopped once to have a meal at a wayside restaurant, fill up the truck's tank and change drivers. Daphne was dozing when at last they reached the outskirts of Mexico City and didn't really become alert until the truck stopped.

Looking out, she saw squares of coloured light which seemed to hang in the air and realised they were hundreds of windows in the dark concrete blocks of apartment buildings. Soon she was in one of those apartments on the fifteenth floor and was gazing down in awe at the city, which spread like a giant bejewelled animal across the shallow lake of Texcoco.

The apartment was simply but comfortably furnished and had two bedrooms. Tom gallantly gave up his room to Daphne, insisting that he would be quite comfortable in his sleeping bag on the big divan in the living room. During the next few days, with his help and Diego's, Daphne learned how to get about the vibrant but confusing city, finding it a place of contrasts where skyscrapers seemed to hug beautiful baroque Spanish churches which were only a few steps away from the ruins of Aztec pyramids. It was truly a city of three cultures; Aztec, Spanish and the offspring of the union of those two, *mestizo*, the modern Mexican.

Traffic jammed downtown streets, Indian women peddled handicrafts along streets which boasted some of the finest shops in Latin America. Elegant gourmet restaurants could be found next to small quick-service cafés where the poor could munch on *tacos*.

Mostly they travelled about the city on streetcars, but sometimes used the new Metro system, and Daphne soon found that this was the easiset way for her to travel from the Avenue Revolution where Tom and Diego had their apartment to Piño Suarez near the *zócalo* in the heart of the old city. It was in one of the streets near the *zócalo* that she eventually found a job in a beauty salon which catered mostly to the many Americans who lived and worked in the city and had no objection to hiring someone who didn't speak much Spanish. All that mattered was her ability to shampoo, cut and style hair quickly, because the salon was always busy.

The hours were long and the pay not very much, and it was going to take her a long time to save up enough money to fly back to Britain, she thought one evening as she left the salon and made her way to the subway station at Piño Suarez, passing the old Colonial church with the plaque in its outer wall identifying the place of meeting of the 'Lord of Mexico' Montezuma and the conquistador Hernando Cortés in 1519.

But then maybe she wouldn't go back to Britain just yet, Daphne continued with her reasoning as she made her way with hundreds of other workers, mostly from the banks and government offices which were centred in the area around the *zócalo* and down the steps into the subway where there was a charming little Aztec pyramid which had been unearthed like so many other Aztec remains when the subway had been built.

Now that she had found a place to live which she shared with Sandra, the Canadian girl who was Tom's girl-friend and who was also studying at the Institute of Anthropology she could stay, she argued with herself as she stepped on to the train. She had been living with Sandra nearly three weeks now and it was a month since she had left Carlos. Her eyes went blind as memories rushed in, and she was no longer on the train swaying to its movement but was in the square at Micatepec hearing Carlos say: *Send me an address so that I can mail the money to you.*

She hadn't sent him an address, although several times she had been tempted to write to him to tell him how well she had managed without him. She hadn't sent him an address because she didn't want the money. She had wanted to cut the ties with him completely and cleanly and to forget she had been fool enough to fall in love with him.

But he had proved hard to forget, and often she longed to know what he was doing. To her own surprise she often wished she was at the ranch, looking out over the grassland to the distant purple mountains, watching the sun go down in a blaze of colour, smelling the scents of grass and sage on the wind, listening to the chirping of crickets and the twanging of José's guitar and hoping, always hoping, that Carlos would come to her soon.

Sandra wasn't in the small apartment when she arrived there. Guessing that her new friend was studying in the library at the Institute, Daphne began to prepare a meal for herself in the kitchen and was slicing tiny Mexican tomatoes when she heard a knock at the door. She wiped her hands and went to answer the knock, thinking the caller might be Tom.

The door swung open and she stared with astonishment at the man who stood outside in the corridor. He was wearing a grey alpaca suit, a grey shirt and a red tie, and carried a white sombrero in one hand, and was looking at her with unwinking opaque black eyes.

CHAPTER EIGHT

AN impulse to greet him warmly, even passionately, was a strong hot feeling rushing through her, causing her cheeks to glow pink and her eyes to sparkle. It took her by surprise, tingling through her to the tips of her fingers, and she almost raised her arms to fling them around him. Then her glance met the hard blackness of his eyes again, noted the stern unsmiling set of his mouth, and the impulse was checked with a suddenness that made her shudder. She stiffened and her chin tilted proudly.

'Hello,' she said coolly. 'Won't you come in? How did you find out I live here?'

Carlos stepped past her, and she closed the door. They both turned to face each other. He was the same, she thought, tough and wary, with depths in him she hadn't been able to plumb when she had lived with him. He was still an unknown quantity.

'I went to the Institute of Anthropology and

tracked down Tom Hutton. He said you were living here with his girl-friend,' he said. 'Why didn't you send me the address?'

'I forgot,' she lied. 'I've been busy working, so I forgot.'

His glance was sceptical. He put his hand in the pocket of his jacket and pulled out a bulky envelope which he held towards her.

'There it is, the equivalent of ten thousand pounds in *pesos*,' he said. 'I suggest you take it to a bank tomorrow and open an account with it. Now you can stop working and buy a ticket to England whenever you like.'

Daphne looked down at the envelope, feeling a strange chill go through her. Once she accepted the money, once his debt was paid, he would leave. He would walk out of her life and forget her as she had tried to forget him during the past few weeks, and he would succeed where she had failed because there was no sentiment in him. He had managed to keep his emotions uninvolved.

'I don't want the money, thank you,' she said in stilted tones.

'But you have to take it,' he retorted, his voice rasping harshly. 'You agreed to be my wife for a while if I paid you, and I like to honour my debts.'

'I didn't marry you for payment,' she replied, her head tilting back proudly as she looked up at him. 'I married you because . . . because. . . .' Her voice faltered and stopped. Her feelings were too strong to be held in check any longer and they

burst through her control. 'Oh, you know why I
married you,' she rushed on breathlessly. 'They
would have put you in jail if I hadn't, and I
couldn't let that happen to you. I . . . I liked you
too much to let it happen. I married you not because you offered to pay me if I would be your
temporary wife but because I liked you. I didn't
marry you for money, and I . . . I . . . still like
you.'

She broke off, realising that she was beginning
to babble in her effort to convince him. Carlos
didn't say anything, so she glanced up quickly.
The black eyes were regarding her rather pity-
ingly and there was a sardonic slant to his
lips.

'Oh, you don't believe me,' she accused.

'*Dios!*' It was more a sigh of exasperation than
an exclamation as he turned away from her to toss
the envelope down on the divan. Turning, back
he stared at her coldly. 'You're right. I don't believe you,' he said. 'And you should be glad that I
don't. There is your money. You can go back to
your own country now—I will take care of the
annulment. *Adios.*'

He spun on his heel and made for the door.
Raging with exasperation and frustration, Daphne
hurried forward and managed to slip between him
and the door. Leaning against the door, she spread
her arms out on either side of her as if to bar his
way. Carlos stared at her, his eyebrows raised in
haughty surprise.

'What now?' he drawled with a weary impatience that roused her temper.

'Oh, you . . . I think you're the most arrogant, most stubborn and most cruel man I've ever met!' she spluttered furiously.

'So?' He shrugged indifferently. 'Then stand aside and let me be on my way, and thank your lucky stars our brief relationship is almost at an end.' He stepped towards her. 'Excuse me, *por favor.*'

'No, not yet, not until I've told you how I feel— really feel about our relationship,' she said, desperate now in her search for ways to break through his guard. 'I don't want it to end,' she whispered, going up to him, her hands reaching out to his chest within the opening of his jacket, palms sliding seductively upwards over the smoothness of his shirt. 'I don't want an annulment of our marriage. I want it to go on for ever and ever.'

'You don't know what you're saying,' he said through taut lips. 'I warned you at the start that there was to be no romance, that it was to be a business arrangement only, a temporary affair.'

'I know you did. But it hasn't worked out that way,' she argued. 'I want to stay married to you. I want to be your real wife, live with you, have your babies. . . .'

'No, no!' he interrupted her, and paced away from her into the room. Suddenly he turned and came back to her, the line of his lips softening, the hostile glitter fading from his eyes to give way to a gentler almost compassionate expression. 'I thought I had made it clear to you when you were at the ranch that I am not the man for you, that I don't want you to be my *real* wife, and that was why you left with Hutton. You got the message and left,' he said quietly.

'Yes, I did,' she whispered. 'But it was too late. The damage had been done, I'd fallen in love with you. I'm still in love with you.'

'*God!*' He grated the word through thinning lips and raked fingers through his tawny hair as he paced away from her again. 'In love, in love!' He sneered the words and she flinched. 'What the hell does being in love mean? And how can you be in love with a man you've just accused of being arrogant, stubborn and cruel?' he demanded, swinging back to her, his eyes glittering again as they stared into hers.

'Oh, I said that because I was angry with you, because you wouldn't believe me when I told you I liked you. And I had to get you to stop and listen to me somehow. You're always insisting that I listen to you, but you never listen to me. And sometimes you do behave arrogantly when you refuse to take into account another person's feelings; you behave stubbornly when you don't want to believe what you hear; and you're cruel when you . . . you're protecting yourself against love.'

The black eyes widened slightly with surprise, but almost immediately they narrowed warily again.

'What nonsense you talk,' he scoffed. 'And what nonsense you believe—silly romantic nonsense. 'His lips twisted wryly. 'Like a lot of other women you create illusions about a man, make him out to be some sort of hero, then say you're in love with him.' He paused. The mockery faded from his face, leaving it sombre. 'I don't want you to be in love with me,' he said slowly. 'I'm not the sort of man you should be in love with. I'm much older than you are.'

'Only eleven or twelve years,' she argued spiritedly.

'And I've done many things in my life you would not approve of.'

'I don't care about what you did before I knew you. It's what you've done while I've known you that matters to me,' she retorted.

'I'm hardened, experienced. There have been many other women,' he continued roughly. 'And some years ago, when I lived in New Mexico, I married one of them.'

'Oh!' That surprised her. 'What happened to her?'

'She left me after six months. She didn't like living on a ranch, miles away from the bright lights of the city, from the nearest neighbours. She didn't like spending hours on her own. She wanted me to be with her all the time, dancing attendance on her.' The twist to his lips became a sneer. 'Like you, she had created illusions about me. I didn't live up to her expectations, so she left me.'

'She didn't love you,' Daphne argued. 'If she had loved you she would have found something to occupy her while you were busy. She would have wanted to continue to live her own life even though she was married to you. I'm not like her, and you can stop thinking I'll be like her if I live with you.'

'You're not going to live with me,' Carlos replied harshly. 'You're not suited to ranch life or to the climate.' He drew a shaky breath. 'Remember what happened to you when you went riding with Ana-Maria? You nearly died.' He paused again, looking down at the hat he was holding. When he looked at her his eyes were blank and cold. 'Better to finish it now, *querida*,' he said coolly, 'before any more damage is done to you.'

'I know what it means now,' Daphne said inconsequently. They were standing so closely she could smell the scent of his skin and hair, hear the sound of his heart beating steadily, feeling his body warmth radiating out to her. Desire was swelling slowly within her. She longed to touch him and have him touch her, to let passion blaze up between them and consume all reason, all argument.

'Know what what means?' he queried, eyebrows slanting in puzzlement.'

'*Querida*. It means the same as *my love* or *loved one* or *darling* does in English, and I don't understand why you call me that if you don't love me,' she whispered, her hands sliding up his chest to his shoulders again, her face lifting to his in invitation.

'Stop it!' he snapped, his lips curling back in a snarl. 'Stop trying to seduce me.' He stepped away from her. 'I have to go now,' he continued stiffly. 'I'm meeting someone for dinner in a few minutes.'

'A woman?' Jealousy writhed through her like a green snake.

'*Si*, a woman,' he replied dryly, stepping round her to the door. 'Go back to your own country, Daphne. Forget what happened here. Marry someone of your own kind. Marry someone like Tom Hutton.'

'But I don't want to marry someone like Tom Hutton,' she protested. 'Oh, why won't you try to understand? Why do you keep pushing me away? Don't you like me?'

'I like you,' he said between taut lips, his eyes glittering with anger. 'I like you too much to hurt you by demanding that you come back to the ranch and live with me there.' He opened the door and gestured towards the envelope lying on the divan. 'That money cancels your commitment to me. Take it and go. Goodbye.'

'Carlos, please, listen!' She began to move towards him, sensing instinctively that she could defeat his arguments if she could get close to him and kiss him.

'No!' he snapped, and went out through the doorway, slamming the door closed behind him, leaving her staring at the space where he had stood.

He preferred to go and have dinner with another woman rather than stay with her. Daphne ground her teeth as jealousy writhed through her again. Why bother with him? Why not forget all that had happened between them as he had suggested, go back to Wales and find someone of her own kind to marry?

No! Her whole being was revolted by the idea. She had never wanted to marry just for the sake of marrying, and she didn't want to marry now just so that she could say she was married. Anyway, she *was* married, to Carlos, and she wanted to stay married to him no matter what he had told her about himself.

She also wanted to set up her own beauty salon. Her glance went to the envelope on the divan. Going over to it, she picked it up and weighed it in her hand, wondering where Carlos had obtained so much money. Had he borrowed it? Was it a loan from a bank which he would have to pay off? She should have asked him instead of letting his behaviour sidetrack her into discussing her feelings for him. Until she knew where the money had come from she couldn't use it. Oh, there were many questions she should have asked him, about his mother and about the ranch, and all of them would remain unanswered if she didn't see him again.

She pushed the heavy envelope into her handbag and returned to the kitchen to finish preparing the meat sauce for the spaghetti she intended to eat for supper, and all the time her mind was busy, tussling with the problem of what to do next.

Where should she set up her own business? In Wales? As she stirred the sauce she let her thoughts dwell on her homeland, recalling how nostalgic she had felt about it when she had first seen the vast tropical grasslands where the Fontaine ranch was located, and gradually she admitted to herself that she didn't want to go back to Wales. There was nothing there; there was no beloved person there to draw her back.

Then where could she set up a beauty salon? Here in Mexico City? The answer came quickly. There were too many beauty salons in the capital already, vying with each other, competing for clients, and although she had enjoyed living in the busy metropolis there was no beloved person here either to keep her here.

Then where should she go? Into her mind there flashed a picture of the small beauty salon Teresa had pointed out to her in Micatepec. The only one in the town, Teresa had said, where it was difficult to get an appointment because it was so busy. *You could make your fortune here*, Teresa had said to her meaningfully. But she hadn't taken the hint. She had been too determined then to leave Carlos before it was too late; before more damage had been done to her.

She drained the spaghetti and heaped some of it on a plate. How hard Carlos had tried to keep her at a distance this evening, even denigrating himself, pointing out to her his faults. Even his terse story about his brief marriage had been told to put her off, and she could see it explained much of his attitude to marriage and women. When his first wife had left him he had been hurt and he was afraid of being hurt again. Yes, that was it. He was afraid of letting another woman share his life intimately because he knew that such closeness could bring pain and disillusionment. He was afraid he might hurt her, and he liked her too much to hurt her.

With a groan at her own confused feelings she sat down at the table and stared at the food on the plate before her. What should she do? How could she convince Carlos that love and marriage could be joyful and fulfilling? Only by being with him, by living with him, not for just a few weeks but for months, for years, for a lifetime, until death parted them. And how could she live with him if he kept rejecting her?

She picked up a fork and began to eat, forcing her mind back to the idea of setting up her own business. There had been space to rent in the new shopping plaza in Micatepec, near the bus station. She could open a beauty salon there. But she would need help; the help of a good sharp business mind; the help of a native Mexican, and there was only one person she knew who was like that, apart from Carlos. She would have to go and see Teresa as soon as possible.

Once she had made up her mind she didn't change it, and at the end of the following week she left the beauty salon where she had been working, said goodbye to Tom and Sandra and caught the bus for Tuxpan, on her way to Micatepec and the Fontaine ranch. The journey was long and tedious, and by the time she reached the shopping plaza where she had once drunk coffee with Tom her head was aching and her spirits were at a low ebb.

It had obviously been raining all day in the small market town and she had to offer the driver of a taxi double the usual fare to persuade him to drive out to the ranch because he was certain that they would get stuck somewhere on the muddy dirt road to the ranch house. The atmosphere was very hot and humid, and as Daphne gazed out at the flat alluvial terraces of land sloping gradually upwards towards the distant foothills which were fast disappearing as darkness swept over them in rolling charcoal grey clouds, Ana-Maria's words returned to mock her. *It becomes disagreeably hot in the summer and the rain can be torrential. When summer comes you'll be gone. You'll have left Carlos and will be sueing for divorce.*

Well, it was the end of May, almost summer, and she was back, and she had no intention of sueing for divorce. In fact she had come hoping to prevent Carlos from arranging an annulment, thought Daphne, tilting her chin defiantly at the rain which had begun to slant down again.

The taxi didn't get stuck in the mud on the dirt road and they reached the yard in front of the old French ranch house without mishap. Grey gloom shrouded the building and no lights shone forth from its windows in welcome. It was shuttered and dark.

As Daphne counted *pesos* into the outstretched hand of the taxi driver a figure in a sombrero and slicker carrying a flashlight sloshed through the puddles towards the car. The rear door was pulled open and a dark face appeared.

'Señora Reynolds!' exclaimed José Valdez in surprise. 'Why didn't you let us know you were coming today? We would have sent someone to the town to meet you.'

'I wasn't sure . . . I mean, I didn't know I was coming today until this morning and I couldn't let anyone know,' Daphne muttered, stepping out into the rain. Muttering and cursing, the taxi driver was wading through puddles to the back of the car to unlock it and take out her suitcase. She glanced at the dark ranch house. 'Is Señora Fontaine at home?' she asked José.

'No. She does not live here any more. Didn't Carlos tell you? She has retired and has gone to live in the village where she was born. No one lives in the house and we are going to pull it down, build a new one.'

'Oh, no! It's so beautiful,' she protested.

'It's rotten, falling apart, like the family that used to live in it,' retorted José. 'But you are getting wet, *señora*, standing here. Hurry to the bungalow. Carlos is there and he will be pleased to see you.'

'I . . . I'm not sure,' she said hesitantly, pushing wet hair back from her face, feeling water soaking through the soles of her shoes.

'I am,' said José forcefully. 'Since you went away a month ago he has been difficult to work with, sour and ungracious, like he has a pain somewhere.' José's sudden grin was wide and white in his dark face, encouraging, then he swung away from her towards the car which had been started but was refusing to move either backwards or forwards, its wheels spinning in inches of soft wet mud. 'Eh, *amigo*,' José yelled striding over to the taxi, '*que pasa?*'

Realising that her case was standing beside her getting as wet as she was, Daphne picked it up and began to walk round the barn towards the glow of lights coming from the bunkhouse and the bungalow. Rain slanted down in straight sticks, drumming steadily on corrugated iron roofs. She went slowly up the verandah and paused in the shelter. This wasn't how she had planned her next meeting with Carlos. She had planned to meet him again in the presence of his mother and had hoped to tell him she had made arrangements to start a beauty salon in the town. She had hoped to meet him on an equal footing as an independent career woman, quite capable of looking after herself yet still willing to live with him as his wife. She hadn't wanted to arrive like this, like a waif looking for haven from a rainstorm, looking for a place to lay her head for the night. But where else could she go?

She opened the door as quietly as she could and set down her case. Her feet squelching in her soaked shoes, she entered the living room. Carlos was sitting at the roll-topped desk writing something. His back was straight, his profile was as proudly arrogant and self-contained as ever. He looked tough, as if he never had a kind thought or a tender feeling in his life.

'Hello, Carlos,' she said. 'I . . . I've come to see your mother, but José tells me she isn't here. He said I should come in and ask you. . . .' Her voice dried up.

He didn't move immediately but sat looking down at the paper on which he had been writing for at least three seconds. Then slowly he turned his head and stared at her, frowning slightly, his black eyes hard and unwinking as their glance flicked over her wet hair, limp soaked blouse and skirt down to her waterlogged shoes.

'How did you get here?' he asked.

'By bus and then by taxi.'

'Why have you come?'

'I've just told you—to see your mother. I thought she might be able to help me, to give me some advice about opening a beauty salon in Micatepec.'

One of his hands which was resting on the desk closed slowly into a tight brown fist and bone showed through at his jawline as his mouth tightened.

'I told you to go back to your own country,' he said harshly. 'I thought you'd have gone by now. Why the hell have you come back here? It isn't the place for you.'

'I . . . I can't agree with you,' she retorted. 'I've decided that I don't want to go back to Wales. I've decided I'd like to open a beauty salon in the town so I can live and work near where you live and work. I . . . I've come back so I can live with you again. I realise now that I should never have gone away. I should have stayed and taken the consequences of living in the same house as you and being near to you.' She walked slowly towards him until she was standing beside him and could look down on his ruffled tawny hair. Tentatively she put out a hand and smoothed some hair back at his temple, noting that there were silver threads among the tawny-streaked brownness.

There was menace in the underbrowed glare he gave her and he caught hold of her hand with fingers that bruised and pulled it away from his hair. But he didn't let go of her hand as he rose slowly and somehow threateningly to his feet.

'So you want to take the consequences, eh?' he drawled softly. 'You impulsive little fool!' He jerked her towards him, his face darkening with passion, his eyes blazing suddenly, his lips swooping to hers. For a moment only he held back, his lips poised above hers as if he were cruelly savouring the pleasure of tormenting her, then his mouth crushed hers in a painful, punishing kiss.

Her breath cut off, Daphne slumped limply against him as if she had no will of her own any more. Caught and held in that angry predatory embrace, she was unable to respond in any way, and it was impossible for her to show him how glad she was to be there with him again. At last Carlos lifted his lips from hers but he didn't push her away. He held her tightly against him and spoke roughly into her hair.

'*Dios*, if you knew how much I have been missing you, *amada*! You see how it is with me? How much I want you? Do you think you can take it whenever we're together and alone?'

'Yes, yes, I can take it,' she whispered, winding her arms about his neck. 'Kiss me again, Carlos, and again and again. Kiss me all night and let me show you how much I can give as well as take.'

His laughter was gruff, muffled by her hair as

his hands moulded her softness against the hardness of his body and his hips thrust against her in intimate invitation.

'When you have had a hot bath and have recovered from your journey,' he whispered, his fingers sliding through her hair to pull her head back from his shoulder so he could look into her eyes, 'then I'll take you to my bed and show you how to make love, all night if you wish.'

His mouth opened over hers again, more gently and sensuously this time, allowing her to respond, and soon they were clinging to each other, blind and deaf to everything, wholly engulfed by the tide of passion which had swept over them, until someone banged on the door and it was pushed open. Wrenching his mouth from hers, Carlos swore tautly and stepped away from her.

'*Que pasa?*' he demanded, looking across the room at José, who was standing in the entrance regarding them with dark eyes that seemed to dance with mockery.

'We need your help,' said the foreman in thickly-accented English. 'The damn taxi is stuck in the mud.'

Carlos's glance slanted back to Daphne's face. He made a helpless gesture with his hands.

'You will excuse me, *por favor*,' he said. 'Go and bathe. I'll be with you soon.'

She had been in bed some time and was slipping into a doze when he came at last, sliding into bed quietly. But instead of leaving a space to separate them he rolled into the hollow where she lay and pulling her against him smothered her mouth with his while his hands curved to her breasts. Through the thinness of her nightgown his bare skin burned as he pressed against her urgently, and his fingertips inflicted exquisite torture as they sought and found hidden nerves until she was dizzy with delight and aching for fulfilment. Yet still he held back, tormentingly.

'Are you sure this is what you want?' he asked thickly.

'Yes, I'm sure,' she groaned, her body pressing against his in greedy pleasure. 'I love you. I want you, that's why I've come back to live with you.'

'Then so be it,' he whispered. 'I cannot resist you any longer.'

There was pain, and then it seemed she was climbing a mountain. Breathlessly she reached the topmost pinnacle and after pausing for a brief second she jumped off. Joyously she floated through the air, whirling round and round faster and faster until she touched earth again to collapse, sighing and weeping a little because Carlos had given her at last something she had always wanted from him and for a few minutes in his arms she had known what it was to be free.

Once more she was to experience that freedom during the night before they both fell asleep, and when she woke soon after dawn to find herself couched in warm comfort and held closely against him she remembered it with a small secret smile before she turned her head to look at him. He was watching her, his dark eyes lazily hooded and he was smiling too.

'*Como esta usted?* How are you?' he asked.

'*Perfectamente,*' she replied shyly, stretching her legs, luxuriating in the feeling of well-being. '*Y usted?*'

'*Muy bien.* Very good, Your speaking of Spanish improves.'

'Thank you.' Turning over to face him, Daphne studied his dark face, searching for signs of commitment and love and finding only the perpetual wariness. 'Are you glad I came back?' she asked, still needing to be reassured, not satisfied only with physical pleasure, wanting him to say he loved her and needed her.

'*Si,* I'm glad you came back,' Carlos replied, turning away from her on to his back and closing his eyes.

'And you're going to cancel the arrangements for an annulment?' she persisted.

He was silent for a while as if considering how to answer, a faint frown pulling his eyebrows together. At last he murmured,

'If it is what you wish.'

'It is what I wish,' she whispered, leaning up on an elbow so that she could look down on him, feeling the first sweet stirrings of possession.

Was he hers at last? This man who was handsome in a different way with dark eyes and tawny hair, who was supremely *macho* in the proper sense of the word, physically strong and potent, yet still secretive, hiding from the world the great depths of his passionate feelings, guarding his heart fiercely against the invasion of love. How could she persuade him to let her in and share his emotions?

'I love you,' she said simply, desire surging through her again, clamouring to be expressed, and leaning down, she kissed him on the lips.

Her touch was like flame to gunpowder. He exploded into action, and for the next half hour the magic of the night was back as they made love sweetly and sensuously, never hearing the wake-up whistle or seeing the apricot-coloured light of the sunrise stealing into the room, not knowing that the working day had started until the clatter of Bonita entering the house disturbed them. Then, dazed with loving, they reluctantly moved apart.

'We're driving cattle today across the river to the other range,' Carlos told her as he pulled on his clothes. 'I'll be away all day. What are you going to do?'

'I was going to see your mother to ask her advice,' Daphne replied, wrapping her kimono about her. 'But now I'm not sure.' She glanced sideways at him, biting her lip, not wanting to spoil the new relationship she had with him yet wanting to know the answer to a question which had bothered her for several days, ever since he had visited her in Mexico City. 'Carlos, will you tell me, honestly, where you obtained the money you gave me for pretending to be your wife?'

He slanted her a surprised glance and for a moment she thought he wasn't going to answer.

'I obtained it *honestly*,' he said at last, his mouth twisting with sardonic humour.

'How?' she insisted, going up to him. 'Please tell me.'

'I sold the land I owned in New Mexico,' he replied. 'It was a small ranch, my first and my own.'

'Was that where you lived with ... with. ...' She broke off, struggling with the snakelike jealousy. Would she ever be able to cope with the ugly divisive emotion which caused her to hate anyone who had known him before she had? Would it always be a part of her love for him?

'With Ellen?' he suggested.

'Your first wife?' she forced herself to ask.

'*Si.*' His mouth twisted again. 'I lived there with her until she left and after she left. I lived there and worked there until my mother wrote and asked me to come back here to help her. It was a long time ago.' He shrugged dismissingly. That part of his life was over, done with. His attitude made her feel better, and jealousy receded.

'I'd like to give the money back to you,' she said, taking the bulky envelope from her handbag.

'Why?' He frowned at her. 'I thought you would use it to start a beauty salon.'

'I was going to, but I can't. It's yours and I can't use it.'

'It isn't mine any longer,' he argued. 'It's yours—I gave it to you in payment for marrying me.'

'And that's why I don't want it,' she flared. 'I didn't marry you because you offered to pay me. I married you because I liked you. Oh, surely you believe me now, after last night?' Her cheeks flamed with colour. 'And you probably need the money to help you develop your share of this ranch.'

'I don't need it,' he said, shaking his head. 'I'm not poor, if that's what's worrying you. And we won't always live in this bungalow. Soon we'll have a better house, with more rooms, perhaps a swimming pool.'

'Please take it back,' she said urgently. 'If . . . if you don't take it back I'll always think that you . . . you bought me.' She thrust the envelope towards him.

Carlos stared at her in puzzlement for a moment, then took the envelope from her.

'Okay, I'll take it back if it will make you feel better. I guess you convinced me last night that you married me because you like me and not because I offered to pay you.' His eyes glinted with sudden amusement. 'And now that little argument is over let's begin all over again. If you really want to open your own beauty salon and you find it's possible for you to do it in Micatepec will you come to me for a loan, let me be your banker?'

'Yes, I will,' she said, and going up to him she put her arms about him and hugged him. 'I think that perhaps you love me, just a little bit,' she whispered.

'You could be right,' Carlos replied torment- ingly. Beneath her chin his fingers were rough, forcing her to lift her head and look at him. 'Perhaps that is why I've wanted to protect you even from myself ever since I walked into you that night in Acapulco. Perhaps that is why I have to warn you again that it isn't going to be easy for you to live here with me or to open a beauty salon in the town. There will be times when you'll hate the place and me and wish you'd gone back to Wales. You'll want to leave. . . .'

'No, no. I left once and it wasn't worth it,' she cried. 'I've faced up to that reality already and I've decided to stay here with you, to love you and have you love me . . . just a little bit.'

'More than a little bit,' he said gruffly, and against her lips his were hard and demanding.

'I must go,' he whispered at last, putting her from him. He picked up his sombrero, slung his jacket over one shoulder and strode to the door. Opening it, he paused and looked back at her.

'*Hasta luego, querida,*' he said softly, and turning away strode swiftly along the passage.

Until later, my love. No doubt it had been said many times by many men to many women, but the way Carlos had said it to her, the way he had looked at her when he had said it, had been implicit with passion and his hope to make love with her again when they met later that evening. And for the moment, that was all that mattered, thought Daphne as she began to dress. As long as they could share their feelings about each other with each other they wouldn't go wrong, and everything else they did would fall into place.

We value your opinion...

You can help us make our books even better by completing and mailing this questionnaire. Please check [✓] the appropriate boxes.

1. Compared to romance series by other publishers, do Harlequin novels have any additional features that make them more attractive?

   1.1 ☐ yes   .2 ☐ no   .3 ☐ don't know

   If yes, what additional features? _____

   _____

   _____

2. How much do these additional features influence your purchasing of Harlequin novels?

   2.1 ☐ a great deal   .2 ☐ somewhat   .3 ☐ not at all   .4 ☐ not sure

3. Are there any other additional features you would like to include?

   _____

   _____

   _____

4. Where did you obtain this book?

   4.1 ☐ bookstore   .4 ☐ borrowed or traded

   .2 ☐ supermarket   .5 ☐ subscription

   .3 ☐ other store   .6 ☐ other (please specify)_____

5. How long have you been reading Harlequin novels?

   5.1 ☐ less than 3 months   .4 ☐ 1-3 years

   .2 ☐ 3-6 months   .5 ☐ more than 3 years

   .3 ☐ 7-11 months   .6 ☐ don't remember

6. Please indicate your age group.

   6.1 ☐ younger than 18   .3 ☐ 25-34   .5 ☐ 50 or older

   .2 ☐ 18-24   .4 ☐ 35-49

Please mail to: Harlequin Reader Service

In U.S.A.	In Canada
1440 South Priest Drive	649 Ontario Street
Tempe, AZ 85281	Stratford, Ontario N5A 6W2

Thank you very much for your cooperation.

FREE!

**A hardcover Romance Treasury volume
containing 3 treasured works of romance
by 3 outstanding Harlequin authors...**

**...as your introduction to Harlequin's
Romance Treasury subscription plan!**

Romance Treasury

**...almost 600 pages of exciting romance reading
every month at the low cost of $6.97 a volume!**

A wonderful way to collect many of Harlequin's most beautiful love
stories, all originally published in the late '60s and early '70s.
Each value-packed volume, bound in a distinctive gold-embossed
leatherette case and wrapped in a colorfully illustrated dust jacket,
contains...
- 3 full-length novels by 3 world-famous authors of romance fiction
- a unique illustration for every novel
- the elegant touch of a delicate bound-in ribbon bookmark...
  and much, much more!

Romance Treasury

...for a library of romance you'll treasure forever!

Complete and mail today the FREE gift certificate and subscription
reservation on the following page.